It
Should
Be u!!
My Love

......as each day I die for you more.

It Should Be u!! My Love

......as each day I die for you more.

Anshul Sharma

Srishti
PUBLISHERS & DISTRIBUTORS

Srishti Publishers & Distributors
N-16, C. R. Park
New Delhi 110 019
srishtipublishers@gmail.com

First published by Srishti Publishers & Distributors in 2011

2nd impression, 2011

Typeset in AGaramond 11pt. by Suresh Kumar Sharma at Srishti

Printed and bound in India

Dedicated to,
My parents, 7A and a soul pal…

Acknowledgement

Thank you God...

Well! I do not have any long list of names to give them any credit for this book as the credit mostly goes to me itself. But as I am being a human by the time of my birth, I am also dependent.

I owe my sincere thanks to the college faculties, who always believe that the last bencher is not capable of doing nothing, their criticism challenged me to prove them wrong.

I like to thanks all my colleagues at Nikhil Engineering college , who always do their best by helping me to enjoy the life at its peak by bunking the lectures and spending time with Big cinemas.

I like to remember the motivation initiated by Mr. Surendra Jaiswal, owner of a Book Shop and juice centre (in summer only). My heartfelt thanks to my publisher at Srishti Publications, for their valuable suggestions and constant support in all aspects, without him I am not able to bring this book.

Finally I would thank to all the persons who came in my life and gave me the experiences which helped me to write this book.

Part 1

Destiny Views!

The last bencher........

Doon, Doon, Doon........Dehradun...

"Is the bus going to Dehradun" I asked.

"I am shouting for so long cant you hear it, why are you asking?" Conductor said and again started shouting Dehradun.

" you are ridiculous, just say me will it pass through Roorkee?".

Conversation between me and conductor continued.I confirmed with the conductor whether the bus will pass through Roorkee. 412RS was the fare of airconditioned Bus. My seat no. was 12,which was 3rd row from left.It was window seat.Exactly what I wished for.

Conductor asked me for the change of 500rs as I had given him a note of Rs 500 for ticket and did not had any change.

"you all Agra customers just think that, I have some bank over here in the bus," conductor said.

"Why are you behaving like an awkward?" I got irritated.

He said just give me your ticket back, Let me write the remaining balance on it,take it after Aligarh.Rs 88 balance,He wrote on back of ticket.Some one else was sitting on my seat. A tough guy having height approx 5 feet 8 inch, having good muscles, clean shave, white shirt and grey colour jeans of Provogue.

"Hello sir this window seat is mine, can I have it please".

"Oh sure" He replied with a loving tone.

At last on my seat!! now no one can stop me from going to Roorkee, I mumbled.

Oh shit….!

"What happen?" My seat partner asked. "I forget my luggage in the taxi."

"Let's go, he will not be far from the bus", he said.

We both ran from the bus, "a voice came" we are going, we will not wait for anyone". Oh no it's again that stupid conductor.

My seat partner stopped and said to the conductor with a heavy tone, "don't try to move the bus from this place, if it move, then you will be no more".

Conductor agreed with a scary voice.

We both started searching the white Maruti Suzuki wagonR at ISBT Agra.

Somebody poked me from behind

I turned back to see and the driver was standing with my blue color tracking bag of American Tourister.

"I am waiting for you, take your luggage, I have to go." The driver said.

"Thank you and please don't say this to dad", I said to the driver.

We moved back to the bus.

"Thank you too sir," I said to my seat partner.

"No, its ok brother, where are you going?" He asked.

"Sir I am going to Roorkee".

"Ohh, what a surprise? I am also going to Roorkee,"

My seat partner signaled the conductor to move.He was still scared it seemed byt the way he was looking at us. We both laughed on the conductor and the bus started its journey.5 minutes had passed, Bus had left the ISBT Agra. We both are seeing outside the window. time was about 8:05 pm, the lightning of the Agra at NH-2 was looking quiet awesome.

"Sir, at what time we will be there in Roorkee?" I enquired.

"Not sure, but about 6:00 am we will be there, "condition applied" if there is no traffic jam near "Bulandsehar".

"Sir, it's your first time to Roorkee?" I asked.

"No, it's my second time, but you are going first time hmm," he said.

"How do you know?".

"I guessed after seeing your nervousness on your face", he said.

After 10 minutes…

This time he arise a question. "What is your name?"

Sheil, Sheil Sharma...

What is your name?

"My name is Khan". Sorry, I am joking. My name is Arnav Sharma. For what purpose you are going to Roorkee. Sheil?" Arnav asked.

"I am going to do "Industrial training" cum course based on "Embedded system".

"Are you doing b.tech?" Arnav asked.

"Yes,"

"From where and by which branch?" Arnav asked.

"Mathura, Electronics and communication 2nd year,"

Arnav was a production Engineer of a company in U.S.A,He had completed btech from Agra in my branch itself.

"Sir by seeing u at this stage in U.S.A., I think you are great in studies?" I asked.

"No, Sheil it's nothing like that, I am always "a last bencher". Arnav said.

I was enjoying talking to Arnav and time was passing very smoothly.I thought I might be disturbing him,if he wants to sleep and have some rest.But when I asked about it he was comfortable with me and he too was enjoying these moments.He never sleeped while traveling.

“Ohh great, then we can have great fun, I also don't want to waste my night in sleeping.” I said.

“Hey, what do u mean by great fun? Are you relating fun with “Dostana movie”? Arnav said naughtily.

we both started laughing for this joke on gayism.

Arnav said he was my carbon copy during his young days,college days.As he said this I got curious to know about his college life and all the fun he might have did being a LAST BENCHER.I asked him to tell something about his friends and college life.

“don't you want to ask about my girl friends, my college bunks, my bad activities”?

He was bang on.I wanted to know about these things only.Who cares about good deeds!!

“Yes, I want to know, but only if you are interested”. I said.

“Let me tell you,today after meeting you, I am missing all my days,” Arnav said.

He agreed to rewind his life as we went on with our journey.

The first love.

The days are of my 12th class.

"Mom its January and only two months are between in my board exam of class twelve." I said.

"So, what son are you not prepared for your exam?" Mom said.

"I want a separate room for study?" I said.

"You are already living in a separate room." Mom said.

"No, no, I can't concentrate on my studies in my room." I said.

"So, you take my bedroom or the guest room which ever you suit more", mom said.

"No, in all the rooms, I don't feel comfortable for studies, the voice of television, kitchen utensils ringing always, Bruno (my pet dog) always shouting at the main gate as he hate to see human beings other then his family members. I want a room I can't live here".

"Where do you want to live?" Mom asked.

"I will take a room on rent for three months in range of 2 km with our house. it's about my future, I have to do this if here I show irresponsibility, it will create problem for me in board exam."

I somehow tried to convince my Mom to allow me to shift.She suggested me to talk with Dad.But it was almost a year that I have not talked to him.I denied talking to him and went on with convincing Mom.

I left to vidyut nagar colony to play cricket.

(Conversation b/w my father and mother on air)

Mom : "Hello".

Father: How are you my sweet innocent wife?

Mom: Same as 2 hrs before

She answered in heavy tone.

Father: Don't you like, when I call you?

Mom: I like, but 4 times a day.

Father: I call that much because the call rates are cheaper.

Mom:You will never get change.

Father: What about Bruno, what is he doing?

He did not had any other question. To continue his talk with mom.

Mom:I want to talk something about Arnav.

My mother said everything to him in a pleaded manner as my mother understands that I am facing problems.

Father: oh really, let him go if he really wants to study in this manner, but you go once and see the place where he wants to stay.

Mom: Ok, I will, now can I put down phone.

Dad kept the phone.When I came back after few hours of playing I enquired about response of dad.Both of them agreed but she wanted to see the place and what was the rent.

"Mom, I have already seen the house and confirmed the rent,"

"Where it is?" Mom asked.

"it's in Vidhyut Nagar Colony, house no. 12 corner house. He fixed one thousand rupees per month"

Next day we went to Vidhyut nagar colony in house no. 12 with my full bag and baggage. It is 5 min run from my house. My mom talked to aunty and uncle about the rent.

My mom left and asked me to return till 8pm for dinner.

At last Arnav succeeded in room contest. I am alone at my room having one chair, table and a bed. Oops sorry forget to say one thing i.e. one window.

Yes "window" for which I am doing all these, confused.

Oh bullshit, I had not come here for study. Yes, I had not come here for study.

It was a week before when I came in this colony to play cricket with my friend. Manish is bowling and I am at back of wicket doing wicket keeping in the park. Ramesh is doing batting on the pitch as he is known as the best batsman of the colony. Our team scored 100 runs in 12 over and now Ramesh's team is at 96 and 2 ball are remaining. We have no chance to win because the Ramesh is on the pitch for him it's like a baby game.

Manish had also lost hopes of winning but somehow I was trying to increase the confidence by cheering.But frankly speaking I was the most scared person in the team.

Come on, come on man, give him a Yorker Manish, you can do this.

Manish starts taking run up and the ball was full toss, Ramesh hit the ball for two runs now it was 1 ball two runs to win.

I am completely sure we had lost the match, but still as a good player I am not showing this. Manish again starts taking run up for bowling a last bowl. With one eye I am seeing him when suddenly a silver color Maruti Suzuki came inside the colony and stands in front of house no. 11. As the Manish was about to bowl the delivery, my eyes completely moved towards the car and I saw an "angel in white color suit", white color dupatta on her head , her hairs are of brown color, her eyes are dark black as someone can easily fall for it, red lips. It seemed "the world's greatest painter had painted her." It was like fairy tale for me and BANG!! Thc ball had hit me straight on my forehead and went towards the boundary. I fell down but still my eyes were busy in capturing each small sight of that angel. Everyone in the park was laughing on me as I fell down on the ground.

A voice came from Manish "Arnav we lost the match and its all because of you." Where is your concentration?"

"I am here only Manish; I don't know how I missed the ball." After every word my eyes are towards my angel.

Every one is laughing on me, by saying "Hey Arnav you don't know even, how to stand?" That angel was moving towards the park and looking at the chaos she smiled looking at me. Wow!! Her smile made me numbLE I felt like falling on the ground everyday for this moment. She got inside the house no.11. Every one in the park start moving towards their home while I am sitting on the one and only bench in the park, as it was gifted by the colonizer to the families who live there. Manish is also sitting with me on the bench. Manish lives in the same colony. I asked Manish indirectly about that girl, "Nice car", its new model vxi of WagonR probably"

Manish said "I don't know" in the heavy voice as he is very disturbed after loosing a world cup match.

"Hey stop it Manish, why Are u upset? Leave it, it's a game.So, whose car is this?"

"They are Mr. Gupta, new owner of the house no. 11."

"Who else in his family?"

"Not much confirmed but as my mom says "husband, wife, son and a daughter".

(I mumbled softly, yes that daughter Manish; I want to see her pls call her).

"Did you say anything?" Manish asked.

"No, nothing"

"Ok, then, we will meet tomorrow at 5 o'clock in the evening." Manish said and left.

While returning my eyes were continuously on her house but no one was there.Whole night I was dreaming of my angel. her face can't even move for one second from my eyes. She is the first girl for me,maybe my FIRST LOVE.In entire school hours from 8am to 2pm and tution hours of 3 to 4pm I was waiting for evening to play cricket.Rather to see my angel. I reached directly from tuition to Vidhyut nagar colony. I had come before 1 hour in the park and was sitting on the bench from where house no. 11 is in front. My eyes are on the gate, the windows of the house are opened. All the players of the great Vidhyut nagar Colony gathered. The match starts as usual on its time. I am busy in watching house on 11. The house was painted light red color & the main gate is of black color.I was watching minute things as if I willl be a designer in future.An architect.I was staring at her house continuously and was not able to concentrate a bit on match.

Manish shouted "hey Arnav what happen brother, you don't want to play? Are you not feeling well, then go home."

"No, no, I don't want to leave this park."

The match was about to end but today my angel disappeared. My eyes got wet with tears.Depressed!Upset! Tears were rolling down my eyes.As it was dark no one could see my tears.Match ended and as usual we lost. I just moved towards the park exit gate to go back home, my eyes are counting the grass leafs. While going out of the park my eyes are on the house number 11 and just wishing to god that only once please call her, I want to see her.But my luck didn't support me.She disappeared.Maybe she was just a dream. Before reaching home, I had cleared all my tears.

"Mummy, I am completely tired & don't want to eat food I am going for sleep. Please don't disturb me". As by saying this, I shut my room door.

Lying on the bed,Thoughts started flowing in my head along with tears on my face. "why angel, why? Where were you today, I just wanted to see you once"? I don't know, what was happening to me? My eyes had change their face from tears to dream? Once I feel, I don't want to cry and why should I cry for the one whom I don't know? And sometimes I feel I have some relation with that girl. Is this love?

I woke up at 7:45 am & moved for school at 8:00 am.Whole day in school at the last bench of my class, I am busy in thinking that will I see her today or not. Today first time in my 12th class I bunked my tuition & reached to the 8th wonder that is my angel. As usual I sat on, one and only bench of the park & start starring at black color gate, which is the most beautiful architecture of the world for me. It was 3'0 clock in the afternoon 4th Jan. 2hours had completed not a single person or his voice came from the house. Match is about to start when I saw someone on the gate of her house..

"Hey stop. Some one is willing to play," A boy coming out of the house no. 12 , he had weared black jeans and blue t-shirt, fair color, came towards the park.

Manish said, "why are you so caring for him?"

"Nothing, just as player."

"I want to play, if you all do not have any problem." The boy said while entering the park.

Yes, why not? Most welcome! So, you are new at this place?Which class you are in?" I tried to interact with him.

"BSc. 1st year." The boy answered.

Let's start the match, Manish shouted.

We exchanged our names.

Aakash Gupta.

We both were in one team.While I was sitting on the bench with him. I had only one question in my mind, who is that girl? Can I see her? Once please, I will always loose matches from you, please call her!

I was afraid to ask about it still somehow gathering courage I tried.Still failed.His phone rang.

"Hey Akash your phone".

My angel, yes it's my angel, this is the first time...... I hear my angel's voice. For me it's the soft music through which any vampire can be in love with her.

"Arnav, I am just coming with in a minute." Akash said.

He left and again I started starring at that black gate.

After 2 minute Akash came back.

"What's the score Arnav?" Akash asked.

Hey, Manish what's the score? I tried to confirm.

"Its 25 for 2 wickets" Manish replied.

"Sorry, Arnav it's my friend from Jhansi." Akash said.

"It's ok, so you came from Jhansi. So, what's your father do Akash?" I asked.

"My father is in NTPC, Dadri.He don't live with us,at home me, my mom & sister live together in the house." Akash said.

"Sister, what is she doing?" I asked.

"She is doing a course on pharmaceuticals & had completed B.Sc. One year ago." After hearing this, I am shocked mumbling and counting the years, how much old she is from me? And result is 5 years.

Till the match end.

I am just thinking about the person, who have wife more then the age of their husband. And I got perfect counts to build up confidence.

We all were moving back home when aakash shouted for me.

"Yes Akash, what happened?"

Will you play tomorrow also?

Yes, definitely 110% sure

"So, please give me a miss call, when you start the match.I don't have personal mobile, take my sisters number give a miss call on that & give yours number" Akash said.

We both exchanged the numbers. While doing this I felt like king of the world.without doing anything I got the girls number.My angel's number.

And the story goes on.Everyday I had just one aim and that is to see my angel, while playing. But it was not sufficient,that's why I had to take a room in this house no. 12.

I kept my table and chair in front of the window. So that I need not to do any effort to see my angel.The daily routine went on.As the days going on, Akash became my good friend.

He used to say many things about his sister but never mentioned her name.

It's 20th Jan & from 22nd pre –board exam. I am completely nil in every subject. Whole year, I attended tuitions for the sake of attendance and never studied.I don't know how students concentrate in one room when so many things are more attractive then being in a single room and teacher giving lectures.All students in coaching classes is busy in differentiation & integration, but for me all these things are useless,I can easily get all this in my math's book. So I preferred to sit at last bench.A LAST BENCHER. Before one day of my pre-board exam, at about 10:00 am I am sitting on my chair, looking outside to see my fairy tale & here she is on the roof.She came after taking her bath to put her silky red color night suite & dark sky blue towel on the clothes stand.For the first time our eyes met and I was scared & moved away from window.After 2 minutes I came back to the window, but she had disappeared.

Next day five minutes remaining in start of my exam, I am busy for which god I should pray.Finally I decided I don't want to pray. Just give the exam on the name of next student sitting in front of me for "30 marks" the dream of a failure. Answer sheet is in my hand and question paper on the bench. I love the first step to do, while starting the exam that is to fill up the personal data. Because this data is the only thing, while filling that, I am fully confident, no mistakes and no marks deduction. Yes, completed the most important work of the exam. Now, its turn to see the great symbols means the hidden art of student's, that art might of writing her lovers name on the wooden bench, A heart with a arrow is definitely must on the school benches.

"Arnav, "what are you doing"?"

Nothing mam.

"Why don't you start to answer the question?It's half an hour complete, the time is 10am and at 12:30 pm. I will not hear anything at that moment, so start doing fast."

"Yes, mam." I said.

The unwanted, unusual question by teacher is finished. But now I am busy in thinking about last days 10:00am. It might possible today again at 10:00 am, she came to roof for her clothes. Any how after being a great thinker of the world, I have to pass this pre- board exam. I had started to read my question paper.

"Chemistry pre-board examination".

I moved to section – A, it might be possible that section-A is easy. I started reading the question paper pass, pass, pass, pass in every question I had given pass to all questions of all sections. Fully dam, I don't even hear about the topics in the question paper. I am confused, from where I start, for me every section is similar. I don't know why

Vikas is smiling after reading section-A.. I had surrendered ."One hour completed" teacher announced & I am busy in over writing on my class and roll number. Now for increasing my confidence level. I used to see the faces of students who are weak in chemistry. But here too I failed; everyone is busy in drawing the "molecular orbital diagram".

"hey, Arnav did u know the answer of question number 5 in section-A" my class mate asked sitting back to me in a slow voice.

NO.

I asked, did you know first question?

He said, yes.

I came in the middle of the bench & came to head down position, so that I can easily turn back my head and see in the copy of student sitting back to my bench.

I start copying the answers with in 20 minutes I copied 30 marks answers in sitting at the same position. The teacher noticed me and came near to me and said sit straight or I will throw you out of the class.

Now,its first warning given to me. I have one more chance to have a warning; teachers generally take action on the third time. Now, its turn for next classmate, to perform a vital role in getting me passed.

I asked him the questions & attempted of 20 marks. Now my

work is finished I don't need to come in toppers list. 30 are enough for me. I submitted my answer sheet to the teacher.

I came early at home, after having lunch I took my bike & move towards my room, for study as the words told by me to mom. In real my words are "I am dying to see my fairy queen."

I reached my room and without seeing anything else I came close to window and started scanning the house in front, i.e. my angel's house.

The house has a kitchen in front, while entering from the main gate the kitchen window. When some one enters in the kitchen it can be seen easily. My angle came to the kitchen for cooking lunch. I am waiting to see as she mostly comes in the afternoon for cooking the lunch. And she came to cook food. She is doing something on the gas. Her hair are coming and disturbing her a lot in eyes. She is removing her hairs at the side of ears. And here in window, I can't even for 1 second move my eye balls to some where else. She shouted "Akash, the food is ready have it". I moved from the window as Akash might see me.

All exams had same story. Every student wants more and more marks and it is human behavior and it depends on our brain, which is very crazy and trendy full of selfishness.

Once upon a time a wayfarer, who was making a long journey by foot in the hot sun, was feeling tired and sought the shade of a tree to rest for a while. It is so happened that the tree was a wish fulfilling tree. Sitting under its shade, he wished for a glass of cold water for quenching his thirst. To his astonishment a cup of water was placed before him. After quenching his thirst, he felt that it would be good if he could get a bed to recline on and enjoy. Immediately, a bed was provided from nowhere. Then he thought how nice it would be if his wife also was there. In a flash he found his wife there. At this stage, he had a doubt in his mind as to how his wife, who was so far away at home, could come there and thought it might be demon in her form which might devour him. As he thought in this manner, the woman turned in to a demon and devoured him.

This means this is the result for excessive desire, which can be your enemy, with in you. That's why I believe in 30 marks and don't want any more marks.

How ever I had completed my exams with a tough struggle in the examination hall.

Today it's 1st of February. All coaching classes are opened just to solve the problems of students. Schools are closed for the preparation leave as from 1st march my board exams are starting. My school will reopen on 5th February for the practical formalities and result of pre-board exam.

Again as usual having same work from morning to evening, I use to sit at the window and dying to see her once at a day.

Morning 10:00am, 5th February.

I am standing in front of my class teacher.

"What the hell is this Arnav"? 26%, not even pass in every subject. This is the result of sitting at the last bench in the class. What did you do in the whole year? How will you pass?" She has a train of questions. But my eyes are on the red color Timex watch, in her hand showing 10:00 am, my Angels time. Just now she is definitely on the roof.

"Arnav, there is no need to get ashamed in front of me, see in my eyes, don't look down." Teacher shouted.

"Yes, mam," I said while looking up in her eyes.

"Please child study hard. Other wise you will fail."

I assured her that I will try my best and left.

Its 5 o'clock on the same day. There is no one in the park, as exams are coming everyone wants to be Albert Einstein, as usual I am sitting on my chair & seeing outside from the window. I am scared, if I get fail then definitely Manish will say to Akash and akash to my Angel and she will get to know. Then she will never accept me in future as I will be a failure. I had decided to study. I had made a time table for studying & paste it on the wall. Next day in the morning after seeing my angel at 10 O'clock, I move to coaching classes of all three major subjects' physics, chemistry & Mathematics. All my books are new for me. First I went to chemistry coaching classes.

"Good morning sir," I said.

"Good morning Arnav, how's your preparation going on.Any problem in chemistry Arnav."

Complete chemistry itself a problem for me

"Yes sir,actually I am starting my chemistry from today," I said.

"Ok, you mean chemistry revision, well, very well." Teacher said.

"No, sir, I mean chemistry subject I am starting today. Sir, I am complete nil till now. I don't know even "Molecular orbital diagram" which is favorite of everyone's in our class, as it's the easiest and the scoring topic."

"What do you mean? Arnav are you mad. How can it possible? At last minute, how can I teach complete chemistry in 15-20 days? What had you done in the whole year, when I teach you in the class?"

"Sir I always try to understand but my ears used to hear only two words of you."

"And can I know what those special words are?" He asked.

"Sir those words are "listen Arnav"." I said.

"I don't know what are you saying, it means in the classes you just do formality. Is this you have the same condition in all the subjects?"

Yes sir.

Listen Arnav!

"Sir you had used those words again." I said.

"Shut up Arnav, the only thing which I can do for you is you give your board exams as a formality. Don't take the exams seriously. Just give them. After finishing them, from 1st April join a new batch of chemistry, I will teach you in a better way." Teacher said.

"Sir, you are saying I study 12th next year again."

"Yes Arnav,There is no other way out."

I received the same answer from other two teachers of physics and mathematics. "FAIL" was the only word coming in my mind.There was hardly any improvement in studies. Today its 15th and I am busy in seeing towards kitchen. Akash came to my room.

"Hello Arnav. How are your studies going?" Akash said.

"Not good buddy."

I am thinking of asking my angel name as till know, I don't know her name.

"Hey,I had saved your sister number on your name, what's her name? I am thinking to save her name"

"Yes, why not? Her name is Anadi Gupta."

Anadi, the sound starts moving in my mind. ANADI ARNAV SHARMA. I am mumbling with the names.

"Ok, Arnav you concentrate on your studies. I am going. I have some work."

He moved out of the room. After going out from the room, I search the meaning of Anadi and our Google god said it means

"Endless".

20th Feb,now I have to study only. And I changed myself completely.Window was now covered by curtains.. Whenever I miss her, I moved the curtain & see towards the kitchen.I used to study 18 hrs.The fear of failure and losing her made me study more.

1st march 8:00am

From 10:00am exam will start. Now I shifted myself completely at my home. I left that room. My mom is busy in mixing sugar in curd. As its our traditional belief whenever we go for doing some good work.

"Mom all these things are fake. There is nothing in practical."

"No, son it's not like that." My mom said.

I moved for the exams, when I reach to Examination center, I search for the Admit card. Ohh shit it fell down by me in the route I ran and searched for the Admit card on the roads to my home. 5 minutes remaining for the exam to start and I am on roads fully Scared & nervous.

I came back to the examination centre without admit card seeing towards the teacher inside the examination centre, one of the students said it will take 2 hour for the duplicate admit card. it will be issued from the school concern.After hearing the last horrible sentence from the trendy students my eyes got filled with tears.I am seeing towards my watch it was 10:10am.Already 10 minutes late.

A man about 25 year old age is standing on the gate of examination centre; he said "what happen, something missing"?

"Yes brother my admit card & now I will not able to give exam."

"Hey don't worry Arnav," I wondered how he knows my name.

He took out a folded piece of paper from his pocket and asked is this you're Admit card Arnav.

I opened the folds and saw its mine,written with bold letters "ARNAV SHARMA".

Hey where do you get this?

He said, the exam is started, run fast.

I just hugged him & give a kiss on his cheek.I ran & reached to the room. After finishing the exam I asked the gate keeper, where's that man? Had he left some message or his address? He said no. I reached home and the routine started till the end of exams. After my last exam I was desperately waiting for the moment when I will meet aakash.Oops, I mean Anadi, my Anadi. I knocked the black gate. Anadi is standing in the kitchen, she shouted from there.

"Hey, Akash see "Arnav had come to meet you". And she shouted "Arnav I think today you had last exam.Right?"

"Yes," I mumbled very slowly. I could not believe it.My anadi is talking to me? My love called my name for the first time, I didn't answer properly to her question, as in front of her, it's very difficult to say something. Akash came out of the house.

"will you play today akash."

"Ya, off course. I know Arnav you are dying to play cricket."

"Akash your sister knows about me."

"Yes, she knows about you. My whole family knows you. As you are the only friend of mine here."

A new time table is again made by me. From morning to evening whole day at Vidhyut nagar colony to play cricket. My parents had filled some Engineering entrance exam forms.

25th April

I had my first entrance exam. The exam in based on options a, b, c, d. I have to choose one option in that. I use to do secured things while giving exam. Count the letter of my favorite thing & put tick mark. Like ANADI its five letters. Letters a, b, c, d by counting means "a" is the correct answer. I had given all the entrance exams in this way.

28th May morning 8:00am

My result of 12th class is going to be out today. I saw the result & unbelievable result, I got 70% in the Exam. I checked out two times on the computer. I can't believe this, how it is possible. It might be some fault by CBSE.I got 70%.Everyone was happy at home but I don't care of any percentage, because it has no use for me in my love.Next day I have a result of Engineering entrance Exams, completely Not Qualified in all the exams, not permitted for counseling. My father had come to home from job for my admission in an Engineering college by donation or with the help of god "jack" in India. They asked me in which college you want to take admission in whole India, we are ready to give any amount of donation but it should be good as in India every parent wants to give education first to their child before food.

"I don't want to do Engineering.I want to do B.B.A"

"What are you saying?What the fuck, B.B.A? Do you know in our whole family, there is no one doing B.B.A.Everyone is engineer."

I wanted to do B.B.A rather then the B.tech, because there are many BBA colleges in Agra.

"Ok, let's leave everything, say truth why do you want to do BBA not engineering? It's your choice of having PCM, so what happened now?"

"There is a very high level study in B.tech & I can't manage that," I answered.

"So u r scaring from hard work, if in BBA it comes to hard work u will leave that also?" My father given a perfect answer to my comment

No, I will not!

"No, we will not hear anything. You are innocent about your college decision, so we have to do this for you. You have two options one in "MCCRC COLLEGE" in Rajasthan & the other one in NOIDA

"AMITY University".

Now, it's your decision, in which college you have to take admission.

My father is waiting for my reply as the days of admission are going on. And now I m in a very big problem, what should I do now? I can't leave Anadi, as I know I don't have any future with her, and still I can't live without just seeing her

Its 28th July morning 10:00am, my father, me & my mom sitting in a room. I have a newspaper in my hand. My father & mom having a cup of tea in their hand.

After taking first sip, my mom asked "So what have you decided, Arnav".

I didn't reply, showing that busy in reading newspaper. In the middle page an add is given of "NITIN ENGINEERING COLLEGE" Agra, a new college is established this year only.

This time my father asked in a heavy tone, "Can't you hear, what your mom said"

I am reading verbally "NITIN ENGINEERING COLLEGE".

My father said, which, which one… I said, nothing engineering college add is given.

"Give me the newspaper, which college. This "NITIN". is it good don't you think it is new and will not have so much facilities."

"Do you want to take admission in this? Where it is?" Mom said.

Dad said in Agra itself.

"Ohh, good it will be easier for you Arnav, as you don't want to leave the home." Mom said.

"Do you want to take admission in this new college and remains to stay in Agra?" Dad said.

I just heard the last word Agra, A for Agra and A for ANADI & A for Arnav.

"Yes, fine",

Time to be a Civil Engineer

As now it is sure that I have to live in Agra itself. To continue my love, next step is to arrange everything how should I get close to Anadi. She lives in the colony behind my house. Her house can't be seen from the roof of first floor but from the second floor it might possible to see Anadi's house. I had planned everything and design a true model of a new room at the roof of first floor. And within an hour I had completed a great job by civil engineer without a degree. I had given a proposal of room on the second floor of the house in front of my parents.

My mom said "are you goanna mad, we live only 3 members in a house & we already have sufficient rooms and you are saying that you want one more room."

"Mom you know that, it's not possible for me to study at ground floor, last time do you remember because of this only I had taken a room on rent."

Dad finalized the design of room presented by a new Civil Engineer of India.

Dad said, tomorrow I will call Mr. Kalra Upadhya that is one of the good builder.

Next day morning Mr. Kalra is sitting in the drawing room and enjoying the snacks and a tea for free. Dad called me from my room and asked for the room design to show the builder. Mr. Kalra passed the design having one hand with a cup of tea and the other with the snacks. He said, "From tomorrow onwards construction work will be started." My father gave him a Bank Check as an advance.

Within five days Mr. Kalra had completed his job in a perfect manner. After the completion of construction, I had come to market, to buy new furniture for my room. After placing the order of the selected furniture & paying the bills of that to the shopkeeper when I was at Ratanrathi chouraha my phone start ringing.My cousin was calling me.I parked the bike at side of the road.While talking, I was watching the couples who are going in huge quantity as that place has one park for the couples. The next couple I seen on a Honda Activa, the boy is wearing a cap, blue jeans, red shirt, average muscles having height about 6 feet & the girl is looking pretty and she is looking like Anadi, hey stop its not looking like Anadi she is Anadi.

They both are standing in the traffic jam,Anadi's right hand is on the boys shoulder.I could not stop my tears and that moment.I am feeling like some one had beated me with an Iron rod or I had jumped from a high mountain. Without saying anything I disconnected my cousin's calls and started crying at the same place. After two minutes they both had moved from my eyes. Those two minutes are enough for taking out the soul from my body and fire the body.I wanted to die. The complete moment shown me that how much lonely I was. I came back home to settle all the furniture & my luggage in my room. While placing each furniture I was imagining the moment of traffic jam in front of my eyes.

First day of college

Today is the first day of my college, as every student has a dream to have a college and today its mine dream to come across. But hardly am I excited about my first day of the college, my complete concentration is towards the worlds terrible and horrible traffic jam. I reached college with a formal dress of white color shirt and a non plated black trouser.New college,New batch,New faces,I tried to look around for my school mates but there were no one around familiar to me. From the first day of the college boys had found their new girl friends. We reached college after a journey of 40 minutes run on the NH-2. Total strength is about 150 students in the college including 15 faculty members. The bus had entered in the college and in front half of college there was no ground for sports,just few steps from main building there was a five room set with attached toilet with every room named as a Hostel, yes the description of my college is over. I didn't feel anything bad by seeing all this, because I had already faced worst thing, then all this. Every boy is searching for a pretty girl, to make a first step in the procedure of making girl friend and some of them succeeded in the bus itself they are known as true Engineers.. All students are sitting on the chairs in the main hall; sorry I can't say it as a main hall because it's the only hall no other hall was their in the college. All the students are waiting for the inauguration ceremony. Mostly the students are busy in thinking, what will be refreshment after the ceremony. A well dressed smart man had come to the stage, he introduce himself as a teacher of Electronics in the college. He told about his past experiences in the different Engineering colleges of Agra. He is trying to waking up the confidence of the student in a very sweet manner as "don't worry now you are the victim of this Engineering college you have to suffer it till last" but mostly the student and the front seater in the hall is busy in seeing towards the left side room from where sweet smell is coming, everyone is excited to have food. And here the electronics teacher said the last words "now "Mr. Amit Tiwari" our honorable Chairman Sir will speak some golden words to all of you". He is a 5'3" had weared black color Raymond Suits, the color is matching with his face. Mr. Chairman came on stage and picked up the mike in his hand, but it was not working. One of the peons was called and with in 5 minutes it was ready. So he started his introduction as business man from Bihar, he started two lines in English and rest of them in Hindi mixed with Bihari language

"Good morning students" Every one replied for good morning.

He said, "As you all know we have a new college," but every college is new at the beginning". He discussed about some more colleges that they have no building at the campus they used to study under tree in the beginning and the boring lecture like "for study we don't need building we need enthusiasm and we will create in all of you". So now let us all pledge that "we all "NITINIANS" make so much effort that we reach the goal that no one can say "see it's a new college" in the first year itself".

Now respected chairman sir will continue & he moved from the stage. I am sitting at the last chair in the hall. Just waiting them to finish all this. But now Mr. Chairman has a responsibility to squeeze us. The introduction continues from each faculty member to peon of the college. Its 2 o'clock we had seen classroom & the college get off at 2:30 PM. And the waiting for refreshment is finished and we move on to outdoor of the college and seen a well cooked food is placed, I bet it was not supposed by any one of the student present over there. No one had waited for anyone and star eating the food. I reached home at 03:40 PM. As I reached home everyone was curious to know about the new life which had started today.An engineers life. My dad just gave me a look.He had to leave for job. Taxi is ready & the driver is blowing horn & my dad is ready to move. My father said to my mom "don't give any pressure on Arnav as he has so many loads of studies". My grandmother had also come to our house to c-off my dad. She lives with my uncle at distance about 5km for from my house. My father shakes his hand twice & get in the taxi. When he closes the door I just felt someone slaps me on the face as I had fooled him. I was ashamed while thinking of my dad that he wanted to give me admission in a good college but I made him fool. My whole family gets inside the house, my grandmothers plans to stay at our home for few days. She is very kind,caring and loving.

The game of destiny - 1

Next day in the morning, I woke up at 7:45 AM as I have to move at 8:00 AM for college bus.Not a single minute I used to waste. In the morning I don't have so much time to waste in bath. As I know the value of time and water.Just kidding! I hate water.

Hey, mom you always wake me up late.

Yes, son off course. I am a fool shouting from 6:00 AM on your ears to wake you up but no, you want to make a fastest record in dressing up.

Ok, mom stop giving lectures on dressing time, I kissed on my mother's cheek & said bye.

Take care son, make good friends only.

The thing which I am hearing since 12 years of college.I was late again and bus was waiting for me.Driver was annoyed and warned me. I silently took my seat without saying anything. About 2 km from my stop there is a railway track & the gate was always closed,whenever I used to cross it. Today again it is closed. I just move out from the bus & stand near the gate. I am watching the people standing opposite to me and concentrating on a white color "Honda City". A well dressed man in doctors uniform, is standing near a car.He is looking like 40 – 42 yr old man and suddenly He crossed the gate & came near the railway track & watching the train both side. Someone had stolen his wallet from his pocket.The man who stoled the wallet hit him hard on the face and his specs fell down.He started bleeding. Again the doctor tried to run & caught the thief but his leg got inside the gaps between the tracks & he fell down on the track. His shoe got struck very hard in the track, he is trying to pull it out, but he didn't get it out from the tracks. Now everyone starts shouting, "hey come out, one train is coming run, man run". But no one is going near to him as the train is very near to him, then I didn't seen anything & jumped from the gate. I saw the train is about only 200 meters & it is in a speed about 60 km/hr. I am fully scared, "should I take the risk or not". The driver of train busy in blowing horn. I came near the man and start pulling his leg out from the tracks, but it hardly moved. The man is shouting "help help". But no one is interested in playing the game of "Aamir Khan" of "Ghulam". The face of the man is full wet with the sweat and a fear of death can be seen easily on his face. The train is coming more nearer to me, the man is seeing in my eyes and said leave me and save your life. While hearing this I saw the broken iron sticks of his specs near by him. I picked him up and made a cut on his shoe & tear off the complete shoe. Now the train is about 50 meters far from us the man is just busy in remembering the god by closing his eyes. I make his leg straights put out from the track. Now the train is just 5 steps from us, I push the man to the opposite side of track's I remain on the opposite side. Now every one there has a pleasant smile & saying me "you had a great job", I am just mumbling fuck great job. I am going to die & you all are watching me as a movie, cant you come for help. Till the train crossed the gate, I got in the bus. One teacher stands and asked me, what happen beta, outside everyone is shouting? I said, Nothing sir a puppy had come on the track that's why every one shouting. The railway gate opens & after boring 40 minutes we reached to the college. I had not discussed with anyone about the incident. Today in college again whole day as usual I had spended on my favorite last bench and it was fully boring. Actually the last bench has many qualities like no one is going to disturb you while in between in your lecture sleeping and the other functionality you are the king of your empire at any time you can have anything like drawing on the bench, if you are hungry you can have your lunch in between the lecture. So I think the last bench should be named and land marked as "Multifunctional bench". Teachers had completed 1/4th of the syllabus. Whenever I try to concentrate on studies in college, my brain directly goes towards "Anadi". In between the classes, some times I just think, "will ever I get a chance to talk her in the life"? After thinking this much only, my eyes get full of tears. Three weeks of college days had completed, till now I have no friend in the college. I use to sit at my favorite last bench of the class room. I had made one "Classmate" copy for all the lectures to be taught in college. One day in the college, there is a first lecture of Electrical Engineering. A tall 6'5" man is standing in front of the class & teaching the first topic as a revision KVL & KCL of first Unit. He noticed me as almost one complete month is going to over but I had not raised a single question in the subject.

"Hello, the last bencher stand up."

While standing I am scared as if he asked me anything, how would I answer. My toes are vibrating, but I have to stand and answer. "Yes, sir."

"What's your name boy?" He asked.

"Arnav, Arnav Sharma sir."

"What? Shall I call you sir after your name?"

Everyone in the class laughed on his statement, as if, he is appointed for the "Great Indian Laughter Challenge" by Shekhar Suman. No, I don't mean that sir. I said.

Ok, so did you know which subject I taught you?

Yes, Sir.

Which one?

Electrical Engineering, Sir.

Can you define KVL & KCL, the basic thing of my subject?

I tried to see on the board, it was written "Kirchoff voltage Law" & "Kirchoff Current Law". I said only this much to him.

"Hey, it's only the name define it?" First time I saw in his eyes, as now he wants to insult me anyhow in any condition. Here's I start defining.

"KVL & KCL" are the Laws given by Mr. Kirchoff for some practical use, but I showed my stupidity to read it in the books of Electrical engineering's and wasting my time for the two words to be written in front of my name i.e. "Er" after B.Tech."

"Arnav, mind your language you are standing in front of the teacher? You want to say that whatever we are studying is all rubbish."

"No, its nothing like that, I hate engineers and it's my personal problem."

Every one in the class seeing me with expression as if shocked.

"Why do you hate Engineers? They are the one who making your life comfortable."

"Yes, by doing their work, they are making 100 people's life better and destroying 1000 life."

"What do you mean by destroying 1000 life?"

" Earlier while making one transformer 50 people were required for cutting the sheet, but now because of bloody CNC machine laser cutting technique all 50 people are dragged away from the factory and only one engineer is required to operate it. The result is same,earlier also we get transformer & now also we get transformer."

In a very bold manner, I finished my talk. The teacher is starring me with a bad look saw his watch and said the time is over you can have your lunch. All student in class starring at me and mumbling with their seat partners about me. After sometime everything got normal and students had chosen their groups, with whom they have to do all stupid things while the college time like talking in the free lecture, lunch , toilet, library work etc. Everyone is having their lunch in a group. I am sitting alone on the last bench. A boy came near me & said, "Can I sit here"?

Ya, off course, I said.

"My name is Mukesh,"

"ohh nice name brother, my name is Arnav."

"Ya, I heared that in the lecture. You are really superb & true at your voice. We both opened our lunch packs & start eating by sharing with each other while having food, Mukesh said "Can I sit with u".

I said "ya, why not! But I think you should not sit with the student who had just fought with the teacher, it might effect on your internal marks."

"Yes, it's true, but how can I ignore the kind hearted person, who is much more caring for the 50 workers whom he doesn't know."

I laughed on his statement and said welcome brother to my last bench.

Mukesh had come from Kanpur. He had completed his 12th in Kanpur it self. His father is a government teacher in a school. After completing lunch in between lecture me and Mukesh are busy in talking. We exchanged our mobile numbers before having the college off. In evening time after coming back from college to home, I used to go on the roof of second floor of my house, from there Anadi's house is visible but I can see her only when she come on her house roof. She always comes in the evening at 6 O'clock to take her clothes from the roof. Today also I am waiting for 6 O'clock. And I saw her in a pink color top's matching gown with the top. She is not looking less then a dream for me. I know that she is not mine but my heart don't believe this. One more night I had spended with her thoughts, Next day in the college While entering in the class every teacher had one question on his tongue, "who is Arnav Sharma"?

Mukesh told me all are asking you for your behavior in Electrical Engineering Lecture. Everyone in the college believes that, I am a sardonic, who don't mean anyone, my days in college are getting worse. My first semester is over. I had given all my exams on the basis of last 10 days study. My ten days leave after exams started and I used to go at Vidhyut Nagar colony for playing cricket but my aim is not to have fun in playing but to give some relax to my eyes after seeing Anadi.

8th Feb, evening 4 O'clock.

The match is going to start; my eyes are at Anadi's house. On the left side of Anadi's house, there is a house in construction. Labors live in that house those who work there. From there loud noises are coming as some one is fighting. By hearing this Anadi came out of her house. All the persons standing in the park are seeing the labors. They are fighting because the husband was drunk and he spent all the money in it. No one came in front to help him. When I reached home I just thought of those children who had done nothing. So why do they will suffer for their father? I took some of the old books & went to one of the book shop to sell them. By selling them I got 500 Rs. I come back at home & in the evening at 6 O' Clock time I went to give this money to that family. But I was hesitating to give it due to father's self respect.I used a trick. I dropped the note of rupees 500 in the grass in front of their house very cleverly, so that no one can see me. After two minutes I came to that house and I picked the note, when the labors family is watching me. I said loudly "whose note is this"? No, one said anything I get in that house and said that "it's yours I found it in front of your house".

Their sadness changes to the hilarious moment of life. After seeing the smile on the face of the lady sitting in the corner I felt relax.

9 February, evening 4 o'clock.

Last day of playing cricket in the park from tomorrow onwards my college is opening. We had started playing, everyone is concentrating on the match and I am concentrating on Anadi. She is standing in the kitchen; I don't know what was she doing? Most of the time, when I used to play cricket, she is standing there. The match ends everyone gets back to their house. Its 6 o' clock in the evening as usual at that time I am on the roof. Today both Akash and Anadi came on the roof. I got down and bended on my knee, so that, they will not see me. But I am watching them from the hole in the wall. I saw that, Akash showing my house to Anadi. I am scared and got back to my room. I thought she had seen me, while I am watching her last day.

My phone rings one "a new message for u" with this cute ring tone. I seen a message from Anadi's number.

"Hello, what r u doing?" In the last it was written from Akash.

I replied "Nothing just preparing bag for college."

After that no message.

The game of destiny - 2

Whole day in college, I was just waiting for the message.But no message. When I was coming to home, one boy about 10-12 yrs old is standing on the side of a road and he is crying. In front of another man standing having age about 30-35 yrs. he is shouting on the boy. First I thought the boy and the man are son and father but When I went near, I saw that the boy is well dressed and looking from a good family background But the man is looking like a lower class person. And this thing hits on my brain. I turned around and asked the man "what happen Mr.?"

he said nothing "you mind your own business".

I asked the boy "Do you know this man?" he didn't answer anything.

I wiped his tear and hug him and asked "what happen, who is

he?" he said "bhaiya I was coming on my bicycle and he was on bike .When I came near him my bicycle slipped due to the sand and I fell down. He saw me and tried to stop the bike, but he too fall down on road and now he is saying me, that his bike got stuck off due to me and he wants all the price for the damaged bike, to be repaired. When the boy finished his last sentence the man pulled my hand and pushed me towards the road.

He said get lost from here "I will take his bicycle and sell it off". I am too scared with him as there is no one else on the road and the man having good muscles. First I pleaded him "please leave the boy, and he is innocent and small child".

After hearing this, he shown his leg and said "see this" this is done by your small child, the leg was full of blood.

I again pleaded him and I said "I will give you 100 Rs for dressing your leg. But please leave the boy.

He agreed. I kissed the boy on forehead and said "go home".The boy was happy and thanked me. I started his bike and the men sat behind. He told me the route to his home and we reached. When I gave him the bike keys, he asked for the money. I said "ya off course" I took out 100 Rs and gave to him.

He said "what is this?" give me 1500 Rs for the bike, so that I can take it to workshop.

I said "what the fuck?" are you mad? He gives me a tight slap on my face. My college bag pulled down to the road from my shoulder. I bend down and tried to pick the bag, he kicked me with the leg, like a football player. I don't have guts to stand and fight with him. Next was a punch on my nose. My nose starts bleeding. I am seeing towards the road and at the house for help but it seem that today is some curfew. His family members are seeing but no one is coming to stop him. I sat on my knees and wiped the blood from the nose. He came with leather belt in his hand and shouted give me money,you allowed the boy to go away. I stood up and caught his neck with my left hand and gave two punches with a right hand on his nose. He is flat on the road. The entire family member came near him and trying to wake him up. But the man is just mumbling stop the boy. I will kill him. I picked my bag and sun on route to my home. No one stopped me as I was looking like a "Mike Tyson".

14th Feb Sunday Valentines Day

The morning starts with a thought that today Anadi has a very special date with his bloody boyfriend on a fucking "Honda Activa". whenever I just think of that boy, I feel that "he is my enemy, who had not done anything with me ?" but ,he is the only one who had taken my everything ?. Today I am on a stage thinking that, "if I have a life then it should be with Anadi, if life is not with Anadi, I should not be in this fucking world." My heart should only beat for Anadi, no one else. My breath should only be felt by Anadi other then me. I always feel "one day she will leave everything for me and pick my hand to spend whole life with me".

4 o'clock evening

I am getting ready to see Anadi, oops sorry to play cricket. I had kept my mobile on table and stepping out from the room. "A message for you", oh, no who is that? I don't KNOW why but when I pressed the button "open message" I feel it's from Anadi. I opened the message, it was written "a very happy valentines day to the most chocolatY boy of the world." No name was written. I replied "same to u, but who r u?"

After 1 min "a message for u" my heart started beating abnormal.I opened the message. "Your friend." I am confused it might possible, that the person is Anadi but if it Akash, then its trouble.

I started my next message as "hey Akash, so how's your valentines day and how's your valentine"? And I pressed the button send.

I wished it was anadi. Again a message beeps; I opened it with my shaking hand. "I am not akash." This times my heartbeats 10 times faster. I replied "ohh really, then who are you?" again a message came "I am Anadi".

I have a doubt that Akash is making fun of mine. I replied "Kidding with me, Akash hmm".

Again a message come, "I am Anadi, if you don't believe come on the roof". I hung up, my blood started circulating in the Arteries & veins at its highest speed . I move on to roof of my Second floor, I saw on Anadi's roof, there is no one. I waited for about 2 minute but no one had come. I turned back to get down from the roof. I seen that I left my room keys on the boundaries, I again step up for the keys, this time there is some one standing on the Anadi's roof &

waving his hand towards me. Hey it's Anadi my angel, my fairy, my love, my Anadi. I saw side ways, that some one is watching me or not. There is no one; I had given a single wave from my Right hand & got down to the room. When I got down in the room a message beeps, "Believed or not".

I replied

"Does Akash know, that you are talking to me"?

She replied "No, can I call you?"

I am flying in the air as someone said me you have a Lottery of Rs 1 crore but in real it's much more than that for me.

I replied "OK". My phone rings "Love me the way u want me to, I just wanna be close to u", the cutest ring tone heard ever in my life. I pushed the button Answer.

"Hey, how are you? Arnav."

Hello, I am fine. How are you?.

"I am also fine, had you enjoyed the valentine with your girlfriend?" She asked.

"No, I don't have girl friend & you." I said.

"No, I did not enjoy today," she said.

Why, what about your boyfriend?.

"I don't have."

"Oh really, you know I hate liars and I don't want to hate you," I said.

Really, I don't have.

"I have seen you, with some one", I said.

when, where did you see me? She replied as if scared.

"About 5 month ago."

"Ohh, then he is definitely "Nimit" on Honda activa." She said.

Dinner or Disturbance.

"Hey, Sheil are you bored?" Arnav asked.

"No, No, what what happened? Why you stopped? Please continue or I will kill you."

"Ohh, don't do that, who will be there to talk about Anadi."

"Ya, don't worry, I will not do anything before you finish the story. Please don't stop what did Anadi say, about that idiot Nimit? And did you tell about your love to her?"

"Wait wait, I will tell you everything. Don't you feel hungry?"

"Yes a little bit, but not much hungry as compared for your story."

Arnav said, "we will first take dinner, then continue with the story."

"Ok and I have to take 88 Rs from the conductor."

"Had we crossed Aligarh?" I asked to Arnav.

Arnav called the conductor & asked when the bus stops? We have to do dinner?

"Within 10 minutes we will reach Aligarh there is a Restaurant, we will stay their for 30 minutes." Conductor said.

I shown my ticket for the remaining money.

After 10 minutes the bus stops at restaurant named "The restaurant" we both & all the passengers had taken dinner along with the conductor & Driver. The restaurant is fully A.C. Arnav and I booked one of the centre tables and order the food by discussing with each other.

I am just thinking about the heavy paid tax on the food, the bill is on the table of Rs 250. I picked the bill and taken out the complete amount. Arnav stopped me I will pay the bill; you are like my small brother. I still tried to give the money at counter but he pulled my hand & paid the complete bill. I told Arnav that because of me you get a big dam of Rs 250.

"Hey stop it Sheil, don't say this lets go the time is over all the passenger had already went inside the bus."

"I said Arnav pls don't feel bad but please please continue the story, I am dieing to know."

"Yes off course". Arnav said.

Story again begins by Arnav

"Yes, that Honda Activa." I said.

"Nimit is not my boyfriend, I am engaged with him". Anadi said.

"So when you are going to marry him & leaving your new friend," I said.

"Don't worry, it was break up due to dowry, his family wanted Rs 5 lakh cash but my father can't afford that much amount. So it was all finish.".

"Do you love him?" I asked.

"Yes, But now it does not mean anything, Nimit is a married man now."

"Thank god, do you know? What I am thinking?"

"What?".

“The Dowry system should be continued for the long time in future”.

Hey Arnav, please don’t make my laugh now,what about you? Who’s that great girl, whom you are dating today on valentine?

The girl doesn’t know, that she is great? I said.

What had you not proposed her? She said.

“No”

“but why?” anadi asked.

“today I talked to her for first time.”

“Ohh, Hey listen Arnav I m dropping the phone, the balance is going to be over with in seconds” she said.

“Don’t worry, I am calling you”

“ No, no not now, I will talk u late night about 10 O’clock, when every one at home sleeps.” She said

First time in my life, I knew the importance of mobile phones. Now, I m just wishing that the hours changes in minutes & minuets get changed in to seconds. Now its 6 O’clock she will talk at 10 O’clock. I m just starring at watch No work nothing just waiting for 10 O’clock. It’s half an hour remaining for 10 O’clock and now these 30 minutes are getting over like 30 hour’s. Now 15 minutes remains, I am nervous now if she didn’t talk to me or she forgets to talk with me. 5 minutes remaining & I called her tring, tring, tring................................

No one receives the call & my eyes filled with tears. I am sure, she will not talk to me now, when I was about to cry loud a miss call came, it's Anadi. My all the teeth blinked like a tube light & I just called her, in one single ring she received the call. She said, at that moment Akash was in her room.

"Ohh, I thought you got bore with our last session." I said.

"No, it's nothing like that, so you are telling about the girl, why don't you propose her?" She said.

"I want her to feel my love first and then I will say her about my love," I said.

"Ohh good, can I know who is she?"

"Yes off course." I said.

"If I say you are that girl.?"

Ohh, Again kidding, she said.

"Yes I am joking Miss Anadi,"

"Yes, I know. Hey first of all I want to say "thank you very much" she said. "Ohh don't be, my call rates are cheaper on Reliance to Reliance," I said.

"Stop it not for that", she said.

"So, for what? For helping the labors on that day with Rs 500",

"No, I didn't do anything, that note I found in front of their house," I said.

"Ohh really, but I saw someone putting the note in front of the house & then doing the drama. But I think that "someone" doesn't know that there are much clever people in this world than him.got it Mr. Arnav," She said.

"How you saw me?" I asked.

"I was watching you from kitchen window, but I don't understand, why you did not give the note directly to them," she said.

"It's because, if I give them the money directly, then his children's feel that, "their father is a failure doing beggar job".

"Ohh, Mr. Arnav is really very smart." She said.

"Oops, you mistaken I m not Smart its enough to be Arnav I said. So, Miss Anadi anything planned about Mrs. Anadi". I asked

"No, not now, it's all I leaved on destiny" she said.

"But you have to choose your life partner," I said.

"Yes, you are right, but I don't how I can marry some one, whom I don't love or trust? So I leaved everything on my parents."

"Hey, you had not said me about that girl, who is she?

"Which girl?."

Whom u love? She asked.

"I can't say her name,"I said.

"Ok, but where she lives?" She asked.

"In my heart, I saw her first time & she made a well furnished 3

BHK house in my heart I tried to get far with her but I can't As there is one law in love logy? I said.

Law, what law? She asked.

The one who wants to get far that much is directly proportional with her closeness to her, I said.

"Hey! Why do you want to get far?" She said.

"she don't love me.she is older then me." I said.

"So what? It doesn't mean anything, no time for love? If I was in place of her, I will never say no to you, Arnav I just want to know truth who's that girl? Other wise I will not talk to you anymore?" She said.

"Hey! What happened? Don't get upset! Leave that matter, so how's Akash?"I tried to change the topic.

"No, don't try to make me fool? Who is that girl?" She shouted.

"If I say that is you.........

'Due to Lack of balance your call is been disconnected' Ohh shit, I just throwed my mobile on the bed and switched on my PC I logged to the recharge website & made a 100 Rs recharge on my number. Today I want to salute all the wireless technologies. I called her again, ring goes on, no one responds. I am scared that Anadi got angry with me & will never talk to me. I closed my eyesand thought, I am the one who ended his love story before starting. Whole night I am busy in fighting with my self, that "why I said that she is that girl?

My whole day in college just moved on thinking about that "what will be the next?"

Next day, it's 9:35 PM in the night. I don't know why I feel that she will call me? And correct at 10:02 PM it's a miss call from Anadi. I called back with in seconds she received the call in first ring.

"Hey, how are you? Last night, my mom came to my room, that's why I unable to receive your call". She said.

"Ohh thank god, whole night and day I am feeling that you are angry with my last talk" I said.

"No, if you are not interested to say the name, I will not force you anymore". She said.

"No Anadi, it's not like that?" I said.

"Arnav I want to say some thing, from the time when I saw you giving money to labors I understood your kind hearted behavior, I was dying to talk you after that day." She said.

"Hey don't die, I am always yours" I said.

"Really, don't you leave me as every one leaved me," she said with a true emotional voice.

"Anadi what happened is something wrong?" I said.

"Arnav, I feel that you are the one whom I am waiting since long, please don't go away," she said.

"Anadi are you drunk", Please say the truth?" I asked.

"Arnav, I am not joking, I am in love with you." She said.

"Hello, Anadi what are you saying?" I said.

"I know that, you love some one else, but what I feel for you. I told you. I don't ever allow you to go far from my heart. I need u. I love u Arnav," she said.

"Anadi I m fully shocked. I don't know what is going on. I have two things in my mind.

1. You are kidding with me.

2. If you are not kidding then only I will say about love," I said.

"What do you think Mr. Arnav, only you can give Goosebumps to the person, see how, scared you are? Relax baby I am joking no need to say the 2nd point." She said.

" But Anadi I want to say something truth." I said.

"Please Arnav no more kidding,

"Anadi you are the girl, whom I love, you are the one who made 3 BHK in my heart, and you are the one with whom I am in love at first sight. You are the one who made my nights to day. I know that you don't feel anything for me but I love u darling and always do". I said.

"Only one thing. I want to ask after your long proposal Mr. Arnav,that how do you know that I don't feel anything for you."she said.

"I am not kidding anadi,I am serious".

"What are you saying Arnav? I mean, I love u my fool & want you to be mine forever." She said.

"Ohh really Anadi I don't believe this, oh my god you are there in world to hear the voice of true lovers, thank you so much god and thank you Anadi my sweet angel I love you. Anadi do you know for today I had prayed in front of every god, I am sure one day my love will be completely mine". I said.

"I don't believe that you love me so much, thanks Arnav for loving me truly, I don't know if I deserve or not and today is very special day for me, I got two thing one I got you, my dream man & second I got a job from tomorrow I have to join."

"Hey, Anadi see its 5 o'clock in the morning the time is passing in seconds, I think you should have some sleep for 2-3 hour as today is your first day at job".

"Yes Arnav you should also have some rest as you to have a busy schedule in college."

"Ya off course baby, so meet you in the evening at your roof."

C-C Case.

Morning 8 am in the bus.

After having an unbelievable night with my love, I am feeling a different world and just don't want to get free from her dreams in the day time also. As usual on the railway gate the college bus is waiting for train to pass. At the mean time I and my classmates are standing outside the bus near a "Hari Medical Store". Rahul whispered to Mukesh, "Hey that's Man force Condom" Mukesh told see that girl on the packet.

"Ya some one said very true the girl looks awesome while nude, can't we see the packet near by", Rahul said.

"No, it will be bad to buy that, what the shopkeeper will think about us", Mukesh said loudly.

I heard the last sentence of Mukesh and I am in a mood that one "who had won the world war?" no one will think anything. Rahul do you want to see that packet.

He said "yes", with a smile as he is going to have a girl for night.

"Ok let's go & buy", I said. Rahul & I both reached to the counter of "Hari Medical Store". The man in the shop is busy in having Agarbattis in front of the goddess poster as it's the morning time.

I said loudly "Hello give one man force Condom". He starred us with his brown eyes; he is giving a signal that come later on, this time is for prayer. I shown him 20 Rs. notes instead of 5 Rs, he stopped every thing and said "Laxmi Mata want to come, how can I insult her in the morning", the shopkeeper said.

He gave us the condom. Mukesh shouted "Come on guys the bus is moving" I put the packet of Man force Condom in my pocket & ran towards the bus. I, Rahul & Mukesh all three were sitting on the last seat of the bus as I am too excited to see it which I had not seen ever.Today everything looked beautiful and confidence was all over me as today I got my love and I am looking to a new world in front of my eyes.

Rahul mumbled, "hey Arnav, please give it to me, I want to see that" Mukesh starred at Rahul & said "Can't you wait for sometime".We will see it in college toilet."

"Hey don't worry Mukesh "nothing going to be happen" I said.

After this, I pulled out the Man force Condom from the pocket & gave the packet to Rahul. Both Rahul & Mukesh got busy in analyzing the figure made on the packet imagining "how it looks in real?" and I am thinking to do everything without any fear. I started blowing the condom with air. After filling it to the last stage, I wounded it with a thread taken out from the seat cover. I had given the condom a shape of balloon and start playing with it. All my college mates start laughing on me. They all are seeing back towards me. From the second seat near the faculty seat Ajit, Akhilesh and Sumit mumbling in between them loudly that see "Arnav is playing with condom".

When the shout reach on its peak both my seat partner who is busy with the poster girl seen me & shocked "Hey what are you doing?"

"Are you goanna mad? If some teacher sees, then you will be rusticated from the college."

" Don't worry all teachers are sitting in the front. From the seat behind Ajit, Akhilesh and Sumit, Astish is sitting the man having a big boom for cricket," he shouted. Hey "Arnav give me a catch".

I thrown the condom towards the boy and with him a gap of one lady faculty is sitting. Obviously at these times people fail to prove that they are good in sports and Astish had shown me the example. He missed the catch. Now the Man force Condom is sitting in the lap of Electronics female teacher having age about 25 yr ready to thanks this precious thing. She picked the condom, but the condom slipped from her hand and got out of the window as it was of chocolate flavor more sticky.

She shouted "what rubbish?" who is behind that? Everyone in the bus shouted "Arnav mam" by seeing the entire students, I am feeling that today is my birthday and everyone is wishing me "Happy Birthday Arnav".

The teacher said "Arnav you are fired". Meet you in the Director office. The bus entered the gate of IIT, sorry to the gate of "NITIN ENGINEERING COLLEGE". In the first lecture "Ram Prasad" the peon of Director we use to say him second Director Came to my class and announced "Director Sir is calling Arnav" every one mumbled "today he has a last day in college".

The same Electrical teacher is taking the class and in this semester he is teaching "Electrical Machines" to us. As usual I am sitting at the last bench, he said go Arnav. I didn't say anything and moved out of the class. While in the route to Director Office "I am just thinking, that I will tell about all this to Anadi, she definitely have fun". When I reached gate, I just thought about how to defend myself, so that I get relief from this problem, I smiled after getting an idea & entered "May I come in sir"

"Yes come in" Director said. In a very humble manner

I said good morning Sir and good morning mam, the lady teacher is sitting in the office. Total three persons are there in the room. Mr. Director and the Electronics madam who caught me.

Director said "What you had done in Bus Arnav"?

Nothing sir, I said.

"But mam is saying you had misbehaved in the bus."

"No sir, I was just playing with the balloon in the bus & by mistake it got on Mam. For that I am really very Sorry Mam. I will never play with balloon in my whole life. Really Promise mam. Sir, Promise to you also."

She shouted "No that's not balloon." I had seen a shame on her face in saying to director of age about 40 yr the clear word condom, And that shame I made it my weapon. Director said then what's that Arnav?

"Sir that was balloon, I am collecting them to tie in our Auditorium for "Republic Day" really believe me and what else can it be mam?"

"I am not shameless as you are," she replied. Mam

"you are crossing your limits, I had already said sorry." I said.

Director shouted "don't fight like children. Go from here & do your work. And don't ever think of repeating this type of activity again.

I said ok Sir & mam said "sorry Sir" because she has to continue his job till she uses that product.

We both came out of the room. I seen towards mam & smiled. She didn't response anything towards me. I came to my class. Everyone mumbled, what happen? Are you going back home? I said, I am not punished every thing is fine. I am free from condom catch case (C.C. Case).

After reaching home in the evening I saw Anadi at her roof and we passed the smile till half an hour while seeing at each others face. But I am not satisfied with this activity I am waiting for 10 o'clock when she use to call me. And as usual she called me at 10 o'clock and I narrate her complete story of today's drama of mine, she enjoyed it. After seeing her happy with all this I feel confident to do more of these kind of activity. I had also told her about the railway track where I saved the life of one man.

Result of first semester.

Next day in the bus after having a night with Anadi on phone. My eyes are small like a cat and in way to have dark circles. I want to sleep anyhow; I had planned to sleep in class. Today in bus everyone is discussing about the result. I shouted "what 1st semester result is out"? Mukesh said "don't u know late night it had came like a storm, 25% result of our class."

" What is mine result? I asked

Mukesh said, "I don't know".

"What about you Mukesh?" I asked. "I got 4 backs." He replied.

I laughed & said Congrates man. Mukesh said "let us se in college "How much you have"? You will definitely get 5 backs."

We reached college & opened the website, entered the roll number, It was one back. Mukesh was shocked to see that and questioned me.I promised him from next time I will compete you in 4 backs.We both laughed and moved in class.

Every teacher is very well known about my behavior & condition in studies. They all were sure that after one year, I will be out of the college, means I will be year back holder. But seeing my result I got only one back, the dream's of many teachers is been destroyed. As for year back university has a condition of having 7 back in the complete 1st year. And now it's impossible. My whole day in college had going in thinking about the last night talking with Anadi and when the last night talk finishes, I start thinking of about talking which is going to be held in tonight session. Only one week is left for my 2nd semester university exam & I am nil. My night goes in talking to Anadi & days in thinking of Anadi. Today my whole college day is spend in planning my first Date with Anadi, as every boy has a dream to have his girlfriend on a date and the most important thing amount of money to spend on that date from bikes fuel to restaurant bill. It was totally summarized and calculated amount is Rs 500 and I do have only 50 Rs not even for the fuel it should be 100 Rs note. At that time in college last lecture was going on and a notice had came. "All the faculty members and student of Branch Electronics and Communication 1st yr are informed that "Personality development program" is going to be held. Interested students give their name after submitting the 100 Rs as fees". I heard 100 Rs my brain starts working and a voice came from inside "Arnav Can't this personality program have fees 600 Rs, who is going to ask you"? why, why not? It is possible. Done after reaching home, the first thing which I told,

"Hey, mom a very very important personality development program for 2 days is going to be held in college and everyone have to attend that, its fees is Rs 600."

"What 600 Rs for 2 days?" Mom said.

"Yes, very great personality is coming for taking the class." I said.

"Who? Bill gates, that much fees?" Mom said.

"I don't know who is going to come? I need money it's important." I said.

"Ok, take it in the morning." Mom said.

"And one thing more tomorrow I will go by bike to college, I have some work on the route." She said do what ever you want to do.

The dream of first Date

As usual I am waiting for 10:00 pm by leaving my every work. As the clock reaches 10:00 pm, my heart beat start beating fast, I have a fear in my heart will she call me, it might possible she didn't get time to call me or it might be Akash in her room. But the phone rings correct at 10:00 pm. I received it, in the first ring. The first thing I told her is "I want to take you on date". She said "what"?

I said, "yes date, don't you like to meet me."

She said, "yes I too want to meet you, but your college."

"Hey I will bunk, can you bunk your office for tomorrow."

"Why not my love? Anything for you."she said in a very romantic manner .

I told her about my plan. She said ok, I will meet you at 9:00 AM near Firaylal chowk (this place is 2 Km from our house).

We confirmed our plan. Whole night we had discussed about the date and planned many things. Its 6:00 AM in the morning & we both had not taken a sleep for an hour. I said Hey "Anadi you should take some sleep, because whole day you have to be with me."

"Ok sweet heart you should also take some sleep, I will call you when I reach "firaylal chowk" she replied.

As the long wait was about to end I was standing in front of the "firaylal chowk" on my red color "Bajaj discover". Again and again I am watching my mobile screen for "Anadi's" call. This time it rings, I received the call "Hey sweetheart where are you?"

"See opposite of your road, I am seeing you". She said.

When I turned my head towards her my eye balls were shocked. "a beautiful girl wearing white salwar and suit with matching sandals, is looking not less then an angel is waving her hand towards me".

After seeing from the distance only I got the answer, "why should I love her?" she is crossing the road with a smile on her face as we are meeting first time and very crazy to feel each other. She came near me and given her hand in front of me for shaking. She asked "How are you my dream boy?" Hey stop "Anadi", I Said.

"What happen Arnav?" She asked.

"Anadi I am feeling nervous with you," I said.

"Ohh shut up why do u?" She replied.

"I don't know but at this moment I am worried that I have to care for my love whole day, would I do in a perfect manner." I said.

"What are you saying Arnav? I know I am fully secured with my love, with u, I don't want anything except you," she said.

I pushed the button named self start as this is very crazy at that time to start my "Discover" to discover a new love story with a great age difference. While riding I am quiet & very smartly I adjusted my side view mirror to see her face. After 10 min she said said "Arnav if you finished watching me in the mirror will you say something my dear".

"No, no I am not watching you, anyway Anadi its 2 minutes run of "SRK Restaurant", we will talk there. We reached the restaurant and selected the corner table as we are the first customer in the restaurant only staff is moving. I said, this is my first time in this restaurant.

"So why here? Do you know it's good or not." She said.

"No, its fine the weekly contest of perfect hotel is won by them always in whole Agra." I replied.

I opened the booklet and with one hand I am touching my wallet whether its there in pocket or not. Anadi said "order whatever you want to eat, I have enough money.don't think that your love is poor."

"Ya my love I know you are professional but it's our first date & I will pay for everything." I said.

We both were seeing the booklet and anadi was quiet as she understands situation of student. I pleaded her to order something.

She said "I don't have any choice; you are the only choice of me".

I ordered "two Double Sunday ice cream" both vanilla flavors 110 Rs each. Its 220 Rs I counted in my mind after adding 100 Rs of petrol its 320 Rs. now the remaining amount will be Rs 180. We both are having ice-cream of Rs 110. I am feeling nervous how to start talking.

Anadi said "What happened Arnav?

"Don't you feeling bad as you are sitting with a dumb boy friend, who doesn't know how to react with a girl on a date, but in real I don't like these entire restaurants sitting like a poor fellow, who don't have something to do creative".

"What? So what you want to do creative? Sex with me." Anadi said.

"No but anything else from this dumb activity. Ok, let's go where you want to go in Agra for fun." Anadi said.

"Really will you go to the place which I like," I said.

"Lets finish ice cream & move on." She said.

We moved from that place & I parked my bike in the fete. She shocked what? You came to fete? Yes, come on. I said with my long steps and hand in hand with her. I buyed two tickets of "Giant wheel".

"Arnav No I will not go. Please leave me".she said

"No you should go, don't worry I am with you". Her face turned to red. But still moved to the seat. She closed her eyes and picked my hand with her both the hands. As the wheel start moving she doesn't react and gave me a smile. Hey Arnav it was not so typical. And the wheel come to its peak & starts coming down she shouted "Hey Arnav my stomach, Arnav stop it Arnav, I will kill you Arnav" & now at the lower position she said Arnav you are very bad.

I said "Anadi darling enjoy the ride just see in my eyes & feel my hand in hand that I am always with you". she said "ok lets try".

This time when the wheel came to the peak, she start seeing in my eyes & tighten her hand with me and we both start shouting "wowed" hurrah" wowwww.

Anadi shouted Arnav I love you on the first down of the wheel & at the next down of the wheel I shouted Anadi I love u 2. And we both start laughing. The wheel was stopped after complete 10 rounds.

I asked Anadi "How my choice is, is this better then "double Sundae" or not."

She said, "I love you Arnav."

My eyes were with tears, with a thought if she goes far from me I can't live without her. Anadi asked what next Arnav.

I said, have you done shopping in the Mall. Yes many a times she replied.

Let's do together, I said. We parked our bike on the road side. We both get in to a mall. I had taken a big basket of full size from the counter.

Anadi asked "what you will do with that."

I said; "just see the man standing at the helpdesk in the uniform. Do you know he have a work to help customer while buying the accessories. But see he is busy in having cool air from LG 1.5 ton air conditioner."

"So what will you do with that?" Anadi asked.

"Anadi you help me to fill this basket with the things which you like," I said. We start from Men's cloth section three T-shirt & 3-Jeans of different cost from different place. Now to ladies section Anadi say which jeans & Top do you like, 2 day you complete all your wishes of buying costly clothes. She putted 4-Jeans & 8-Tops. Hey good job darling I said. "Ohh sweet heart, thank you."

Now to shoes & sandals section, we had taken three pairs. Now turn to 2 kg sugar, 4 kg rice of Basmati, 2 kg of simple, ½ kg Haldi and the list goes in basket. Anadi asked now what? Anything left for shopping from your side Anadi, I asked.

She said no, it's enough.

"Ok then leave the mall I am putting these trolley's in the corner," I said.

She goes out & stands near the bike & after 2 minutes I reach there.

I said "now that helpdesk member will do his job perfectly by putting the things from basket to its right place".

Anadi said you are stupid & we started Laughing. We are roaming on the bike, my side view mirror is showing my loves face. Anadi is busy in laughing on the previous activities and while laughing she put her hand on my thigh. I am taking long breathes, she asked what happen. I said nothing. And here's a speed breaker, after crossing she tied her hands on stomach. "Thanks to government for putting breaker". And I am feeling that her hand is a part of my soul. But in real she is much valuable then my soul. I took her left hand in my hand, which is already on my stomach and said "Anadi I love you darling please don't leave me alone ever". She replied, "ohh my poor baby I am always yours, no one can take me from you."

I said, "yes sweetheart I too want this. Arnav I want to give you one thing." She said.

She took out a platinum ring from her bag on the bike it self.

I said. "Hey darling it's so beautiful, it would definitely be costly. Why did you bring that?"

"Not much beautiful and costly then you sweetheart it's for you," she said. "Then I should also give you a ring and we will buy it now of your choice".

I stopped the bike in front of jewelers. I counted my remaining money it was Rs 150, I said you choose the one you like, I will pay the cost some other day. We got in to the shop. We asked for the platinum rings for ladies.

The man shown us 10 – 20 rings, every one cost above 200 Rs as the label attached on every ring. I told Anadi, you choose the one you like most. She mumbled in my ears, they all are very costly, we will take it from different shop this is "Ramganga jewelers" they sale costly then others, "Madan jewelers" are very good and give 50 % discount.

"Anadi, just choose the one you like most, we will see later on for the cost."

She chooses one of the rings from 20 rings. I asked this is final. She said, yes.

I mumbled in her ears "the keys are in the bike, just round once for ignition and press the red button on right side to start I am coming".

She gets tensed and was sure definitely Arnav is going to do something typical.

And she saw in my eyes with her scary face towards me and I said slowly go sweetheart and she leaved the shop. I faced towards the shopkeeper and asked the cost of that ring which is in my hand. He said 300 Rs fixed rate. From the window I saw Anadi had started the bike & standing near of it, with fully tensed face. I taken out 150 Rs from the pocket and gave him. I said put this money rest of the money I am bringing from that girl & I shown Anadi from window. I kept the ring in my pocket. He said ok go.

The guard had opened the gate for me and my eyes are on his gun. When I am leaving the gate one of the shopkeeper said "Hey Mr." where is the ring. I said in a very sweet and calm manner "don't worry it is with me".

He said ok fine. I move on towards the bike, I had not seen once towards the guard and that window.

I went near Anadi and start doing acting of opening the chain of her pursc. I mumbled while doing this, see the guard is seeing me or not, she said "yes and from the window also one man is watching."

I said "after count three, as early as possible sit on the bike".

She completely feared and said in her poor voice Arnav I really don't want this ring, Arnav don't do that take money from me, you will give me later on.

I start counted 1, 2 & 3 go. I sat on bike and Anadi too, as she don't have any other option except to accept this. The man shouted "Guard" run he had not given the money catch him. But at that moment we had crossed 100 meters, I turned back & waved my hand towards the guard & start showing the tongue to him. Anadi shouted, "Arnav are you mad can you imagine what they can do with you if they catch you?"

I said, "the rising sun and Mr. Arnav can't be stopped ever."

Anadi shouted, "Mr. Arnav is my foot."

"Sweetheart please don't be angry with your baby, see how beautiful ring it is".

"No, Arnav first you promise me, you will not repeat this again."

" Ya definitely darling promise, Anadi its 2 O'clock we have time till 5 O'clock.". We both were standing on "firaylal chowk". I asked Anadi, had you smoked cigarette ever.

"No, do you smoke Arnav." She asked.

"No dear I don't smoke but want to smoke once," I said.

"I love smoke,"

she said "But where we should have cigarette it's impossible to have it on bike"

"What you mean by "we" Anadi?" I said.

"My sweetheart "we" mean I too want to try that?" She said.

"Ohh really, don't worry about place just wait here for 10 minutes; I am coming with dad's car".

"Don't you have any problem?" She said.

"If I have then also I will bring it for you darling. I came back to home and parked the bike very quietly & taken out the car keys from my mom's bag. Everyone is taking afternoon sleep at home. I come out of the house, start the car & reach to "Akhilesh pan masala" in between the route of "firayalal chowk" to have two menthol cigarette, menthol because no one can catch us at home, it doesn't smell, I had used my last 20 Rs lucky note, which I am saving from 2 yrs. I reached "firaylal chowk" Anadi came & sit at the front seat. I moved back the car towards Industrial area. This area was full of people at two times in a day one at the morning time & other at the evening time and in afternoon the roads do have only street dogs walking on them. I parked the car at the corner of a big tree.. I said, Anadi I think its perfect place. She agreed.

I burnt one cigarette & we both started smoking the cigarette one by one. She said "thanks Arnav for everything. I am damn sure in my whole life I had not seen a day like today as I have with you," she took out the ring & wore it in to my middle finger, her eyes are full of tears.

She said "Arnav I love you darling." After seeing her in a very emotional mood, I am hesitating to give the stolen ring to Anadi.

Anadi said with a smile, "take out the ring sweet thief otherwise I will hand you over to police." We both start laughing in the car having 2nd cigarette in Anadi's hand. I took out the ring from pocket & wore in to her finger.

I too love u darling and thrown the filter of second cigarette. After exchanging the ring we are very close to each other.

I said to Anadi "Can I kiss u".

She saw towards me & closed her eyes, a mumbling voice came yesssssssss. I came near to her lips & tasted her lips with the French style. While kissing. I kept my hand in her white color suit to feel her breast and come as close as possible. Anadi has still not opened her eyes. This time I opened her salwar & said "Anadi can we sit on the back seat?"

She said in a very lovely tone "yes Darling".

We moved on to the back seat. Anadi opened my shirt buttons & start kissing on my chest. I pulled her up and kissed on her lips. A different kind of sweet smell is coming from her body. I opened her salwar and suit from my full regards. I closed the entire window mirror. Anadi is complete nude sitting in front of me. I came near her and start kissing every where. While kissing Anadi opened my jeans and she tried her level best in having me as a sex partner. We both are complete nude. I told Anadi can I come more close to you darling. She said, "I am yours Arnav no need to ask," after hearing the last golden words We both had crossed all our limits. After spending more then an hour in the car. We dressed up as early as we can. Anadi's first word after moving the car from that tree is "I –pill", I want to buy an I-pill" from the chemist. After hearing I remembered that my wallet is empty, how can I say her.

I said in a very calm voice, "actually Anadi the thing is I don't have money left for anything can you give me money for medicine I will give you tomorrow."

"Its ok Arnav why you are so tensed while saying this, I understand because of me you had wasted your so much money today."

And she gave me a 50 Rs note. I stopped the car in front of "Hari Medical Store" and buyed 1 I-pill. I gave it to Anadi.

Anadi told "Arnav I am fully tired can we go home now".

"ya off course".

I dropped her to "firaylal chowk" & we both took our routes.

The day had gone with Anadi and the remaining gone in dreams of Anadi. I am waiting for 10 o'clock to receive Anadi's call. But today I am in confusion will she call me or not, because in last she said I am tired. It might possible she might sleep early. But still I am waiting for her call and at 10 o'clock she called me. I received the call and said how you are sweetheart?

"I am fine darling and how are you? Hope you had relaxed after coming from there", she said.

"No, I am just thinking about the day we had spended together for me it's impossible to forget you today every moment I am missing you. I am missing your hug, your kiss, your hands on my thigh and every talk of yours", I said.

"Arnav I am scared for you", she said.

What, what s going to happen with me? I asked.

"No, not in that sense, I am feared if you leave me I can't live without you darling, I love you and want you for ever anyhow." Anadi said. While saying this it is very easier to feel that she is crying.

"Don't worry darling I am not going to leave you ever, I am much worried for our relation. For me nothing matters except you my sweetheart," I said.

"Arnav while you first time kissed me in the car today I am feeling that you are the one for whom I am been on this earth, for whom I am been waiting since long. Arnav your every touch to my body not less then a hilarious moment of my life, I want to feel you for ever in my soul. I want to make you my reason for every happiness of mine. Darling I love you please don't leave me," Anadi said.

After hearing all this I am getting much scared for Anadi, if in future we have to get far from each other how would we love. In every breathe I am feeling Anadi. My whole night with Anadi is just gone in tears. We both are much feared for each other as if we get far from each other how can we live? I had my first aim and future plan as to marry Anadi. I don't want anything in my life except Anadi. For me she is my life and I can do anything to be with her.

I told Anadi about my 2nd semester exam and after that I have to go on Roorkee for course on embedded system.

She had told me Arnav you better concentrate more on studies, because it's the only thing which makes your future. But after hearing about Roorkee she got quiet and said "Arnav how would I live without you for so much time. Arnav darling I will miss you too much."

" Sweetheart I am going to miss you in my every second of

day.Darling I know but I and you have to be little bit strong because if you feel weak at this stage how will you cross the difficulties in the future."

She said "yes darling I have to be strong" and we disconnected the call.

Part 2

Trip to Roorkee

Any how with great complexities and treasures I had given my exams of 2nd Semester. Summer vacations after the completion of 1 year B.tech was about to begin from tommorow. College announced 30 days vacation and everyone was planning to spend these days with family and relativesBut I planned something different.Full of excitement. In the evening I called Mukesh and Rahul.We were discussing on conference call.

I asked Mukesh "Are you going somewhere in the vacations."

He said "no, I had planned to stay at home only in these vacations and to prepare for the back exams."

I said, "but the exams will going to be held next year.Ya but it's a golden time to prepare for that."

"hey Rahul what u had planned for the holidays?" I asked.

"Till now it was nothing, but after hearing Mukesh I think he is right."

They both asked simultaneously…what you are going to do in these holidays; we know that u will not waste your holidays in studies….?

"Yes you are right. I m going to "Roorkee"."

Rahul shouted "Roorkee" for what?

"There is an institute which is well known for "Embedded systems."

"you are going for a course study, please don't joke."Mukesh added.

"Yes you are right I am joking that I am going for a course,I am doing it for sake of parents,Else who cares!I am going to enjoy every bit of it.Just fun and only fun."

"Fun what kind of fun," Mukesh asked.

"Once I reach in uttarakhand there are lots of places to visit. My parents will never tolerate me to go for studies there. It's a 20 days course 3 days classes in a week. So only for three days I have to take classes in the institute and other three I will be out of station. I had called you both to invite you for that but I think you are not interested in that?"

Mukesh said, "if I study now for the back exams I will definitely forget everything till the exams".

Rahul, said "you are right Mukesh."

They both agreed join me and I was successful in convincing my partners. My next step is to find out the places for visit near by Roorke.Again technology work, I had searched all the places and selected the days for visit to the particular place. We all were standing on the bus stand of Agra and waiting for the bus to Roorkee. Our parents had come to c-off all of us.We had our tickers booked.As the bus arrived Mukesh's dad shouted to just concentrate on studies there instead of other things.I thought if they were so serious about studies they wouldn't have joined me.But our parents will be parents!!

I get close to my mom and touched her feet, my father had not come, and he is busy on his job. She kissed on my forehead and her eyes showed that she cared for me.

I said" don't worry mom.I will be fine." She smiled.

The conductor shouted get in. we all of boarded the bus and waved our hand towards our parents.Mukesh looked emotional as his eyes were in tears.

I shouted with a big laugh "fuck off man are u mad."

He said "no I m missing my mom".

"stop it u r just going for 20 days out from your home. Don't get emotional like a girl"And we all laughed.

I told them my real intentions and they both said not to force them into anything.It wa perfectly fine with me.

Mukesh said "its 9:00 pm and till 6:00 am we will be there in

Roorkee."

They both slept and I was sitting at the window side, I too closed my eyes.

I was missing Anadi. I messaged her "talk u after 20 days, miss u and the car" she replied "missing u too, take care".

Mukesh and Rahul were unaware about Anadi. I was just thinking of last meeting with Anadi and missing her too much . Whole night I was just thinking how would I spent my days without Anadi.

Its 6:00 am, I asked conductor how much time is left for Roorkee he said "with in 5 min we will be there"

oh shit, I shouted to Rahul and Mukesh wake up we r going to reach. Mukesh said, "mom please five more min,"

"abe tera baap hu.Uth saale". They both woke up and got ready to see the new life.

We left the bus at Roorkee bus stand. In front of the bus stand there was one hotel "Man Singh Hotel" I just knocked the counter,a man had came rubbing his eyes. I said in a loud voice "we want one non ac room for three, do u have it.We want it for 20 days." He had shown a big smile on his face after hearing the word 20 days. After having a great discussion, we agreed on 300 rupees per day.Mukesh and Rahul too agreed to share the amount of money. We all checked in the room because at 10:00 am we have to attend classes. We had completed all my registration process online.

The first day in the institute.

We reached late as usual and teacher had started the class

I said in a polite manner "sir may I come in". He said u r late.

I replied "I had come from Agra in the morning itself."

He warned us to be punctual nowonwards..Mukesh and Rahul followed me. After rotating my eyes in a 20/20 feet room I found a last bench empty. We had sat on it. I m trying to see the blackboard but the writing was horrible, so I tried to listen to the word he was saying, but unluckily it is impossible to listen his voice it was too soft. Mukesh and Rahul were still busy in analyzing the language written on blackboard. I put down my head on the bench and tried to sleep.

After seeing me the teacher shouted "u last bencher stand up."

Mukesh signalled me with his elbow.I got up and everyone was looking at me

"what's your name?"

I said "Arnav, Arnav Sharma."

So u had come from Agra to sleep. Everyone laughed on me in the room. Mukesh mumbled in Rahuls ear "Teacher's game over". I had given a sweet smile to the teacher and came in front of the blackboard and said

"oops it is English friends"

“what do u mean…?”

“Nothing Sir I m thinking u r teaching us in Brazilian language.”

After hearing this everyone laughed on the teacher. The teachers face turned in to red.. Teacher said “u can’t ever be placed in any company ever in your life with this attitude”.

I said, it’s because I say truth….

“go to hell class dismiss, from tomorrow I will continue the class students.” After saying this he moved from the class. Every student in the class starring me as because of me, they cant be engineer 1 day before.Rahul and Mukesh came near me and Rahul said “how are u feeling after insulting the teacher”.

Mukesh said “no he is right, the teacher deserved that”.

From next day every students in the class requested me to stay quiet in the class otherwise the teacher will again leave the room, and the course will not be over in time. So I came and sat at the last bench daily and started planning to next tour in next three days.

It was late evening., Mukesh said “lets drink today”.

Rahul said “no…I will not.”

But I said, “done lets bring it up.”

Mukesh and I moved to wine shop and took two bottles of “Bacardi” costing 600rs each. We both shared the price. When we came back to room, we saw Rahul was crying loudly. I was fully scared and asked “what happen”?

"My father had called me "my dadi is no more"."

I smiled and said " That's it.I thought your girlfriend cheated on you.Forget it.Leave it.Let her go." He started crying loudly

Rahul said while crying "I will kill u, Arnav".

"Its ok Rahul.Chill!"

Mukesh opened the bottle.while taking first peck in front of Rahul I said "cheers to dadi who is no more, dadi pls take care of yourself, Rahul loves u a lot".

After hearing this Rahul hugged me.I consoled him that everyone has to go one day or other.

Mukesh shouted "Arnav take your drink."

I pushed Rahul back towards the bed and enjoyed the drink. After finishing complete 10 pecks, I stood up and said"I announce as I m drunked 9 pecks, Mukesh shouted hey its 10 peck, oops sorry, my friend is correct its 10 pecks, but still I know what I m doing? I didn't have any effect of 10 pecks really.

Mukesh said "yes my friend Arnav is right we both didn't feel that we r drunked, Arnav lets go for a walk its 11:00 pm we will be back at 12:30 am."

Rahul shouted get in front of the truck and go to hell.

I said Rahul, "how could I do that do u forget I had promised your dadi, to take care of yourself."

We both were on the road, Mukesh said, "Arnav I love u it's

my dream to roam after drink like this and u had completed that"

A car is parked near the tree, I said "Mukesh I want to break the car glass." He took the stone from the road and hit on the car but he missed.

I said, "Mukesh let me try u r drunk, I will break."

I too missed the spot.Mukesh shouted "u r also drunked Arnav, why don't u tell me."

I said, "sorry Mukesh next time before drinking I will tell u."

Mukesh took the stone and he hit the glass and the glass was broken. We ran after the glass broke. Someone shouted catch them. But till then were too far.. After broking two more car headlights in Roorkee, We came back to our room. Next day we have to go Massori hill station. We went there by bus. We stayed a night there in Massori for enjoying the monsoon. After having a long night in Massori we had decided to stay one more day in Dehradun, next day we enjoyed in Dehradun. After coming back to our hotel. The owner of "Man Singh Hotel" was standing on the counter, He stopped us. I came in front and asked, what happen?

"You all three are using a single room at a cost of two person."

"So what we had talked to the room in charge in the beginning," I said.

"He is fired yesterday," the owner said.

"It's not our problem; we have a receipt of your hotel".

"No now you have to pay 400 Rs per day or you better leave the room." Mukesh came in front and said "are you mad don't you have any rule and regulations regarding your hotel".

I agreed with the owner.Rahul said "do you know the total amount we have to give is 2000 Rs extra. And we all had wasted in visiting Massori."

"What is the remaining balance of the hotel?" I asked.

Mukesh calculated in his mobile, its 2000 Rs + 2000 Rs = 4000 Rs.

So now we have 2000 Rs more to spend in the market. What rubbish? Rahul said.

"Is it necessary to give the remaining balance?" Mukesh said

I tried to explain them that we can cheat as he too is cheating.But they didn't agree. We had taken our remaining classes sincerely not me but Mukesh and Rahul. Today is the last day of our course; the teacher is presenting certificates to the students. When my name is called I get close to the teacher and said "slowly, thank u for wasting my 20 days here."

He mumbled "Arnav do u remember the thing which I told u...?"

I said "how could I forget that. I will come after completing my b.tech and when I have a job in my hand."

Teacher said "I will wait for u…"after saying this I moved back from the institute with Mukesh and Rahul.

"Hey stop it."

"What happened shiel?"

"Sorry about that but I want to know that why u r going to Roorkee to meet that teacher?"

"Yes to complete my promise and tell him every students future does not depend on any teacher, it depends on himself. Hey Arnav if u want a break take it, we will continue after some time."

"No I don't need that"

We all came back to the hotel from our institute. The owner is standing on the counter; he asked when you are going.

I said after two days and we will clear all your accounts tomorrow. Mukesh and Rahul got to know that I had started my game. After entering the room, I start packing and asked Mukesh and Rahul to pack the entire luggage in one bag, just take out only night dress and sleepers.

Rahul asked me, "what are you going to do?"

I said "now its 8:00 pm, after 1 hour the duty will shift and only guard will be there in the entire hotel. I am leaving the hotel in the night about 1:00 am through the bathroom window."

Rahul asked, "and where do you stay in the night?"

"I am going to railway station. Mukesh you throw the luggage from the roof to the ground at the back of the hotel carefully that guard will not see you. And in the morning both of you at 5:00 am came out of the hotel for morning walk as you do daily and your morning walk end at railway station."

Mukesh gave me a pleasant naughty smile and said you are awesome. Rahul was confused over it but as we did not had any option he also agreed. We all were waiting for 1:00 am and its 12:45 am.Mission begins! Mukesh said after 5 minutes I will be there on the roof with the luggage. I opened the bathroom window and saw outside, I saw that some one is standing and waiting for someone. I got in the room. After 5 minutes again I saw outside, the man is standing with a girl. The man given a 1000 Rs note to the girl and then both went on bike somewhere. I putted my legs outside and with my hands I grabbed the pipe. And by slipping on the pipe I got down to the ground. The complete back portion of the hotel was empty. Only one 100 watt bulb is switched on the road.

Mukesh shouted slowly "hey, Arnav catch it." I waved the signal to throw the bag on road. He threw the bag on road. After taking the bag on my shoulder I started my marathon towards the main road for rickshaw. A man is sleeping on rickshaw, I waked up "get up man, will you go railway station". He said no. I tried the next.He asked 50rs but I made him settle with 40rs. I reached railway station at 1:30 am and there from 1:30 am to 5:00 am I fought world war with Indian mosquitoes. They both reached and hugged me. "You are great Arnav", Rahul said.

We all three came back by first bus from Roorkee to Agra. We all three are standing on the bus stand of Agra and start moving towards the route of our house ,

I shouted, "hey stop who knows we are in Agra, cant we stay together whole day in Agra without telling our parents".

Rahul said "you are mad Arnav, had you not filled your dreams in 20 days want to do more fun. I want to meet my parents; they all are waiting for me, as I had not met them after my dadi's death".

Mukesh said, "let him go Arnav."

I asked Mukesh, "What's in your mind"?

I m planning to have last 2 pecks with my friend who had given me the most unforgettable moments of my life, do u take ?..Why not, I replied?

One Day Marriage

After having the outthought fun in Roorkee today is my first day in college of 3rd semester. As usual I m sitting on the last bench with Mukesh and Rahul. We all three are discussing just about the days of fun in Roorkee. Today morning itself we had reached Agra from Roorkee and came to college. I am dying to talk to my love. But I am not getting a single minute to talk with her. When I came back home in evening I messaged Anadi as I had came back to home and will wait at 10:00 pm for the call. The time is 9:45 pm and my phone rings. I picked the phone its Anadi, "hey love, how are you"?

She replied, "I am fine sweetheart, how are you? I missed you so much darling."

"Anadi my love for you will never change, whether you are close to me or miles apart from me.Without you there is nothing in my life.. Anadi when I was in Roorkee in nights I missed you the most, I hate nights it seems to be long."

"Ohh darling please don't love me so much, it will hurt me, when we get far," Anadi said,

"Arnav when you were there in Roorkee, my maasi had come to our house from Noida. She lived 5 days at our home. She introduced one boy for my marriage. His name is Arpit Gupta. Now he was a lecturer in Noida. He is my maasi's neighbor. My parents had decided to meet him.They had fixed up almost everything. The boy is ready to marry. I told my parents that now I don't want to marry. But they are not hearing me, as the boy's parents are not taking dowry. They want me to marry as early as possible."

"What, Are they fool? , tell them you love someone else," I said.

"How can I say this if they ask who's that?" Anadi said.

"Tell my name, what's the problem?"

"Will your parents accept me?You are Sharma and I am Gupta, I don't think so that they will agree."She said.

"No they love me and I love you…they will agree."

"It's good if they agree but please Arnav do fast whatever you want to do? I can't live with my parents anymore. I need you my love. There is no one who is mine in this dirty world."

"Don't worry Anadi I will try to do something as early as

possible.Now its 3:00 am you better take sleep now." I said.

"Ok sweetheart goodnight I love you".

I closed my eyes with Anadi all over my eyes and soul.I was fully tensed.How can I say to my mom that I love a girl? And I want to marry her, at this age when I am not stable.The Morning alarm woke me up and I went to school without having breakfast Whole day I was thinking of some solution but could find only 1 solution. I had to talk to my mom. Continuously 15 days I increased my confidence level to talk with my mom. Every night Anadi pinched me to talk with my mom. And at last my father had come for 1 month leave. Sunday morning everyone were sitting in the drawing room and watching television the stupid repeat of daily soaps while I was getting nervous. I thought to talk later on and moved back from the room and I heard a voice of laughing. I thought this is the right moment to say everything. I told in a very soft voice "mom" but no one heard me as they are busy in laughing, I don't know what is so funny going on at this time when I am going to discuss about my life. This time little bit loudly "dad" I want to talk something. My mom and dad faced simultaneously towards me. What happen Arnav? My mom asked. My eyes got melted after seeing my mom is asking me like that as I am sure she is always ready with my every decision but don't know will she agree today.

I didn't face towards my parents; I am seeing the blue color carpet written welcome on that. I am thinking once they get yes I will welcome Anadi on this carpet. This time dad said what happen Arnav? You had not answered your mom.

"Dad I know that I am not right while saying this to you. But mom please try to understand me"My complete body wass vibrating. I stopped my legs from vibration and said

"mom I am in love with one girl."

My mom shouted "what are you saying do you know that?" My dad starts giving me a bad look.

"Yes mom I know this but I love her and want to marry her."

My father said "what will you offer her to eat? On my income you will fill up her stomach or complete her needs ?don't you feel ashamed to do that."

mom said "who's that girl?"

"She lives in vidhyut nagar colony,Anadi."

"That girl Anadi Gupta." My mom said.

"Yes my friend Akash's sister."

"But as I heard about her she is 5 year elder then you." Mom said.

"I don't know mom how I falled in love with her. But I love her"

Dad shouted me and almost kicked my ass and went away and mom was left crying.I went into my room and had tears in my eyes.

In the evening my mom came to my room and said,

"you had hurted all of us Arnav, I had never accepted this from you."

"Mom please try to understand me."

Mom left the room and I was not satisfied by my parents views about my love,

Anadi called me in the night and as usual her first question was had you talked about me to your family. I told her the whole story and she gave her expressions as if she knew this would happen.

"But Anadi they are right at their place, how can they get ready for my marriage at this age?"

"So what do you mean Arnav we are wrong by loving each other."

"No I am not saying this. But I can't blame this for my parents, if in future we are in place of them; we we will think the same.We will wait till we get stable."

"Arnav why don't you understand my problem, every day I am fighting with my parents for you.I can't marry some one else than you, it's my final decision. For that I can cross any limits. Arnav do you love me or not? "

"Off course baby I do. I said. Ok then lets run from our houses."Anadi said.

It was impossible to run away as we didn't had a house to live,neaither food to eat.I disagreed with it.

"You want me to marry that bastard lecturer whom I don't know?"

Anadi said.

I told her to convince her parents to wait for 2 years. But she was bit confused. My mobile battery was low so we kept the phone.

Next day as usual I was sitting at the last bench with Mukesh and Rahul. The subject is electromagnetic field theory. As the name of the subject is too long it's too long to understand it.. It's impossible for me to pass.

I received a text on my mobile, its Anadi. I opened the text, it was written "I am going to die, tell me from where I get bus for Haridwar I will jump in Ganga canal". I smiled as I thought she is joking and I replied "from ISBT Agra best of luck". She again replied I am not joking; I am standing on firaylal chowk. I thought of talking to her. I showed as if I am feeling like vomiting and teacher allowed me to leave the class.

I took a bus to firaylal chowk.I reached firayal and saw Anadi is standing in blue color jeans and white color kurta. I smiled but she didn't respond to me. I came near and asked what are you doing sweety?

"I am going to die or you come with me.We will go anywhere but lets move from here Arnav, I can't live without you a single moment darling I need you. I am alone in this world. Now you are everything for me."

"But Anadi please try to understand where we will go." I said.

"Arnav I had saved 10 thousand Rupees and 5 thousand Rupees jewellery, it is enough for month to stay in any city of India and in between 1 month I will get job.Arnav if you are scared or you don't want to come please leave me alone I have to pick up the bus for Haridwar." Anadi said.

"Ohh shut up; please try to understand it will be much more difficult for you." I said.

"I know Arnav but baby I love you and can't live a single moment without you." Anadi said.

"So sweety it's your last decision." I asked.

I agreed with her as I really love her.I was planning to have some help from my friends for residence and a job for me.The first number is of Cousin Anish Sharma, he is an Assistant Manager in an ICICI Bank of Agra. He is 2 years elder then me but we are very close to each other and I am fully sure he is the only person who will definitely help me. I called him.

"Hello can I talk to Mr. Anish Sharma." Yes Arnav how are you?"

"I am fine Anish and how are you?" Anadi mumbled don't waste the time and just come to the point.

"Hello, Anish I have some work with you, do you remember we had discussed about the girl with whom I am in love."

"Yes off course, who is 5 year elder then you?"

"Yes-yes that one. So had you proposed her or not?"

"Yes Anish I did and just now she is with me.but just now I want your help. Anish she had left her home and we had decided to leave Agra to get married in different city."

"What the fuck you are saying Arnav?"

"Anish I know its sounds bad but its truth.I want 5000-10000 Rupees which ever is easier to manage for you, I will return it to you after some months."

"Arnav are you mad how can I give you that much money?"

"Why cant you give, you have a perfect job you can give and I am promising you I will return it to you after few months."

"Sorry Arnav but I can't help you, how can I trust you when you are no more of your parents."

"Anish please try to understand I love her and I want to be with her forever, I talked to mom and dad, they clearly said no and I don't have any option other then this."

No I can't Arnav and he disconnects the phone.

Anadi saw my face with embarrassment and she was sure that Anish had not helped. I discussed everything whatever I had talked to Anish.

"Don't worry Arnav we will definitely find some way."

we took taken a rickshaw for Arundhati Park which is near to Firaylal Chowk. The rickshaw had taken 10 rupees note. We had taken 2 ticket of the park 5 rupees each and this is my last 10 rupees note in pocket.

Anadi told, "don't worry Arnav I have money."

We got in the park and choose the corner seat.I opened my contact list again and continuously called ten old friends, for the world they are known as are my best friends, but today they all are busy.My eyes were in tears after the last call.Anadi picked my hand and said don't worry Arnav I will do something.I will call my cousins who lives in "Firozabad".

"Anadi we can do one thing you go and live to your cousins house for three Days till then I do some arrangement here in Agra for a job and a room on rent in Delhi, what do you think is it correct or not?"

Anadi agreed. "Ok then done you will stay at your cousin's house in "Firozabad" and I will meet you in Agra after three days and don't tell them, that you had ran from your house they might create a problem. Just say that you have a holiday for three days so you had came to visit. Anadi its 12:00 o'clock and it will take three hours to reach "Firozabad". I will drop you till Firozabad and come back to Agra."

We stopped the bus to Firozabad. Only one seat is left in the complete bus, I told Anadi to go and sit on that. Anadi sit on the seat and I stood near her. Anadi took out 200 Rupees note from her purse and gave to me for tickets.He given me ticket and asked for 100 Rupees. I had given him 200 Rupees and asked to get change of 100 Rupees; he had given me the two fifty rupees note. I gave one fifty rupee note to Anadi. She gave me back and said take it, it might possible you need this.

"Had you taken the lunch in college Arnav?"

No, I didn't.

"Ohh then you will be hungry.When we reach Firozabad have some thing to eat. Arnav I know that you are so much hurted because of me and I had given you so much pain please forgive me."

"Don't be Anadi please you are doing this because you love me." My legs are paining too much as I am standing since last hour. Anadi stood up and said please sit Arnav you are so much tired.But I told her to relax.I came in front stands stand on the bus gate.Anadi gave me a call, she said do you know Arnav why I leaved my everything for you before thinking once of my family.

I said because I am very smart.

No it's because you love me so much that you can't give me pain and can have pain for me.

"Ohh really." I said while smiling towards her.

She said by again waving her hand please come near me. I came and stood near her. She said "please don't leave me like this."

"Don't worry baby."

The man sitting next to anadi was getting down from the bus. Anadi pulled my hand towards the seat. She leaned her head on my shoulder and said "Arnav I love you sweetheart."

"love you too darling." Arnav will you marry me right now"

"Stop kidding dear"

"I need you for my whole life as we need oxygen to live. I cant live without you."Anadi said.

"Ohh baby don't be sentimental I am yours forever, I don't need any certificate from anyone that I am married with you or you are my wife.".

"I know Arnav you are always be mine."

"So my sexy wife why do you need marriage drama."

She smiled at me in a naughty way.It was 3am and we both were hungry. I shouted towards conductor how much time is left for Firozabad. He shouted and said 30 minutes.

"Darling it will be too long ,you are hungry lets have some food," I said.

"But the driver will not stop."Anadi said.

I had a plan and winked at anadi and told her to co-operate.As usual she was afraid and was stopping me. But I cant see her hungry.

"Hey stop the bus, its Hunger Attack to my wife please help someone, please stop the bus."

The man standing near my seat asked what happen.

"My wife got an Attack "hunger attack".It's a kind of attack when ever she is hungry she have this attack in this she stop doing everything now she can only see the food, if we get late she will get in "Coma" so stop the bus." Everyone heard the last word "Coma" and started shouting "Stop the bus near the Dhaba". Driver parked the bus near "Punjabi Dhaba". I got Anadi in my arms and seated her on the chair. She is really a good actor she had closed her eyes and had not given a smile. I ordered the best food that I can. I shaked the Anadi's head and signaled to open the eyes and have food. Anadi opened her eyes very slowly as if she really got an attack. She didn't wait for husband to say something else, she started eating the food. Anadi is eating food and she offered me the food by her hand.Everyone started clapping and had a smile in their eyes.We both took our seat and Anadi mumbled thank you husband for giving me the severe attack. After we reach Firozabad. Anadi told me the address of her cousin. I asked from the rickshaw owner he told it is near by from this place I will take 20 Rupees. I gave him the money. Anadi seated on rickshaw and I told the man to move his rickshaw to the address. I kissed on her Anadi's hand and told take care of yourself my wife. She kissed me back.

We both have eyes filled with tears and waved our hand towards each other. I gave her the sign that after you reach call me.

I got back to bus stand and took the same bus to Agra. I am sitting at window side. I am thinking about my mom regardongwhat she will feel, when I will run away from the house. She is the one who had given me the birth; she is the one who knows everything before I speak from the mouth. And again my tears start falling from my eyes.I reached home.My mom said "you are late Arnav."

"Yes mom there was some function in college today."

"So had you eaten food after lunch?"

Mom served me food and I was enquiring about dad.Soon I saaw him coming with Anish. I am sure he told everything to Dad. My dad came near me and asked, "you are late where you are?"

"In college Dad." I said.

"Ohh shut up what do you think we are mad? Dad gave me a tight slap on the right side of the face.

"I love her". I said and I saw towards Anish, he gave me a bad look. I didn't match up my eyes with any of the member. My father shouting, he had done a cheap work for that he should not be allowed for food. After a long time I am crying in front of my dad. But he is busy in giving me slap one after another. My mom came near me and said will you live without me Arnav. And she hugged me and starts crying with me. My father pulled my Mom towards her and said he is no more our son till that girl comes back to her home.

"do you know her family is blaming you all around. Where is that girl?"

I didn't answer anything. He took out my mobile from my pocket and saw the last dialed number it was Anadi. He called Anadi, Anadi received the call "hey darling had you reached home, we all are having party here in Firozabad and my cousin's are missing you"

My father said in loud voice "listen girl I am Arnav's Dad I just want to tell you leave Arnav and get back to home, till you dont come home Arnav will be locked in the room no food nothing to him" Anadi didn't answer anything and my father disconnects the call. Now the next my father call at Anadi's house.

"Hello sir, Arnav had come back and I called Anadi she will be with you till tomorrow morning."

My father locked me in the room. Whole night I did not slept just thinking about Anadi, what she is feeling? How she is? Had she eaten the food?

Next morning a call from Anadi's dad had came that she had came back to home. My mom opened the gate and offered me the breakfast first. I didn't have but my mom had forced me and given me with her hand, while she was offering food with her hand I started crying and said sorry mom but I really love that girl as much as I love you.

"Arnav please understand by doing all this you are not destroying your life, but also destroying Anadi's life. How much you earn without any degree, will you fulfill all her dreams. No you can't. So just wait for right time to come then do all this. At that time we will not disobey you, but at this time it's all rubbish."

"Mom I am not saying that I want to marry her, I will marry her after I get job, but till then Anadi will be married."

"How's this possible she is Gupta and we are Sharma's."

"Mom the true thing is that you all care much for your prestige not for my feelings."

"Arnav we are living in this society so we have some rules and regulations to live here."

"Just stop it mom "is the rules and regulations are bigger then someone's love, feeling's and care. You all living in the fake world."

"Arnav whatever you say is correct but whatever I told is truth and the truth is you can't marry Anadi." She left the room.

I called Anadi but no one responded as my number is saved in her mobile. After 10 minutes again I called her this time Akash receives my call but he did not allow me to talk with her. Next day my father sent me to college and said don't ever try to repeat the same mistake. I saw towards him and left the house for bus stand. Before I reach the stand I called Mukesh to stop the bus if I come late. And as usual the bus is waiting for me. Everyone in the bus giving me a bad look, but not more than the driver. Rahul asked me is everything all right? I nodded. We reached college.Whole day I am quiet in the college. Every teacher is asking me what happened Arnav are you all right? I said yes to everyone. Rahul came near me and asked in the last lecture just tell me what happen? I said nothing brother, my head is paining. Rahul said "the one who always give pain to other's head, today his head is paining it means there is something."

Mukesh had also came near to me and said "Arnav don't you believe us". "No brothers it's not like that," after so much force I narrated them my complete story. They both have eyes filled with tears. Rahul said Arnav what kind of man you are "sometimes you behaves like you don't believe love and sometimes you behave like love is everything for you, sometimes you give smile to the faces and now you are giving tears to the eyes".

When I finished off my last lecture a phone call came at my number from my Mom. I received it,

"hello Arnav don't get down to your stop from bus. "Tandon Nursing Home" your grand mother faced the severe paralysis attack."

I got down to "Tandon Nursing Home". I saw my mom is standing with my aunty (wife of my fathers elder brother). I touched her feet and asked how r u? She replied I am fine but your dadi in the afternoon suddenly got a "Paralysis Attack". As I heard the word attack I didn't concentrate towards my Aunty but my brain directly moves towards the "Hunger Attack" my mom and aunty both are having tears in my eyes for dadi and in my eyes it's for Anadi as I am missing her a lot. My Aunty hugged me and said don't cry she will be fine very soon doctor said. My mom cleared the tears from my eyes and we moved towards the room in the hospital where my dadi is admitted. I saw from outside through the glass she is sleeping. My uncle (my fathers elder brother) is standing outside the room I move towards him to be the most sincere and a religious boy in the hospital to touch his feet. He blessed me and said have some food in the canteen you had came from college. I said no it's fine. My dad said me go get it don't worry we are here. After I heard this from his mouth as he said once a good thing to me after that incident. I felt to hug him but it's not the right time and right place. I move towards the canteen my father shouted wait Arnav "take this bag it is full of grapes I brought for you" after hearing this I cant stop my self to hug him, I hugged him tightly and said in the sad voice

"sorry dad please forgive me, I will never hurt you anymore, I love you dad."

"I love you too Arnav, go and get some food,".

Whole night my whole family stayed in the hospital and next morning the doctor discharge dadi, he said take precautions and medicines otherwise next attack can be dangerious for her.

[illegible]

[illegible] and [illegible] [illegible].

[illegible] saying [illegible] [illegible].

[illegible] The [illegible] [illegible].

[illegible]

[illegible]

[illegible]

[illegible] sorry that please forgive me, I will never hurt you [illegible] [illegible]

got hurt.

"Have you [illegible] [illegible] done that."

"[illegible]" [illegible] finally [illegible] [illegible].

[illegible] morning, the doctor [illegible] [illegible].

[illegible]

The Unforgettable

The months had passed very smoothly I didn't get in contact with Anadi. I tried to contact Anadi with different numbers but I am not successful in contacting her. Every night at 10:00 pm I waited for Anadi's call. But always an eternal feeling came and said "she will call me" by taking this hope I started living my life. My dadi had come to our house for a weekend from my uncle's house. From morning to evening she has a bag full of medicines after every hour she has to take medicine, I am having my 3rd semester external exam preparation leave for 10 days but still my eyes are closed, I am planning to have all studies in between the gaps of the exam. My morning started with a medicine for dadi named in bold letters "Nurokind plus". My mom is busy in cooking breakfast for me, as I want it early. Today is the last day of my preparation leave and from morning itself I had opened my books as tomorrow is my first exam. My books are as new as they were in market. I had studied complete one hour and a call came from my uncle "today is the day for medical checkup.

We reached hospital; the concern doctor is busy in operation theatre, 3 hours are completed in waiting for the doctor but again the lady at counter is saying he is bit busy.I was worried about my exams.I was still virgin in studies.

"Sir please gets in to the room, the doctor had finished the operation" the lady at the counter said.

My uncle steps forward towards the room and told me take care of dadi I am coming. He gets in to the room for asking doctor and as he gets in, he waved her hand towards us from the glasses to say come in. I hold my dadi's hand and took her to the doctors room. After 5 types of tests he told us to move for home and said take the report tomorrow. We got back to home and my uncle dropped me and dadi to our home and left. As early as possible I got in to the room and started studying. Now its 9 o'clock in the night, my mom called me for the dinner, I planned to study after having dinner. My dadi told me at the dinner table, "sorry Arnav for disturbing you for the exam you had wasted your whole day for me." I came near her and kissed on her forehead to say don't be, for you its nothing, I can leave my exam.

"No-never don't ever try to leave exam oeven if I die"

" Dadi please don't say rubbish, I will not allow you to go anywhere before my marriage. And I have to do two marriages. So it means you have to live at most 20 years more."

"Ohh shut up Arnav; I can't wait for that much time, do marriage as early as possible."

"Ok then after exams I will do."

My dadi smiled and said go study for tomorrow. I had completed my dinner till 9:30 pm. I got back to room and checked my cellphone to have 2 misscalls. It was Anadi. Before thinking anything else I just push the call button. Anadi received the call and said I'll call back you in 10 minutes. Akash was there in the room and she disconnected the call. My physics book and Mr. Schrödinger is trying to explain his equations to me for exams in the book, but at the other side Dhiru Bhai Ambani is saying leave Schrödinger and get me in the hand. Now I have to select one foreigner and one Indian, as I believe in nationality Dhiru Bhai Ambani is my choice. I called Anadi after 10 minutes, she received the call and the first word she asked is how you are Arnav?

"fine and you baby."

"I am fine Arnav; please don't use these types of words for me."

"What happen Anadi?" I asked.

"I am going to give this honor to someone else, Arnav I am going to marry someone else. My marriage is been fixed to that lecturer."

"What that bloody Arpit?"

"Arnav don't tell him like this, he is my future husband.Arnav you and your parents will not allow me as your wife, that's why I had decided to get married. For whom I will wait?" Anadi said.

"For me Anadi for me, just wait for 3 years when I get stable we will marry."

"Sorry Arnav once I believed you at the case in Firozabad but you leaved my hand, this time I can't. It's very easy for me to wait 3 years as I am professional and no one can force me to marry, but overall there is nothing for me to wait."

"Anadi why didn't you get in contact me till now?" I asked.

"Arnav when ever you had called me, my cell is with me. But I don't want to talk to you. You are the only responsible for all this;

you left my hand I didn't."

"Anadi how you can say this to me, do you know exactly what happened?" "Yes I know every thing but you are the victim."

"Anadi if you think that I am your victim, then I don't want to prove myself in front of you.Anadi, why did you call me today? If you had decided that I am your victim."

"Arnav I just called you to say that I am going to marry Arpit.after 5 days I have ring ceremony in Noida and after one day I will marry him in Noida itself, my whole family is shifting to Noida tomorrow."

I was numb. I lost my senses. I wanted to shout loud that Anadi you are mine. In front of my eyes everything got black and felt that its end of my life, there is nothing to live in this bloody world. Anadi said three times hello, but I didn't answer anything.

"be happy always darling I love you and will love you always, I will wait for you to get you know how much I love you?" I disconnect the phone and switched off it.

A voice of crying had come from the ground floor of my house. I suddenly got down to the floor and I seen my mom is rubbing my dadi's hand by one hand, from one hand she is having mobile. Mom seen me and shouted call your uncle and say him that dadi is facing attack come soon and call the ambulance. I saw the contact list but Anadi was still running in my mind. Its 25 seconds over but I didn't call him, my mother took the phone from me and called my uncle. Mom shouted on me, wake up and rub your dadi's hand. Now I saw dadi, her eyes are closed and my mom is crying in loud voice and rubbing her hands to move the blood circulation at its normal speed. I am fully scared what is this all happening?

After seeing mom crying, I too started crying. We both are seeing each other but both are hope less to do anything. It takes 15 minutes for my uncle to come at home. My mom shouted just go and call Ravindra doctor uncle. He is our neighbor physiotherapist doctor. I said ok and got out of the house to call the doctor. I am standing in front of the name plate written Dr Ravindra Singh. I pushed the door bell 4 times but no one responded.I searched for other doctors too.But there is no one in the colony to help me.It was too late.It was about 3am.

"Arnav what are you doing lets go to home." Uncle came behind me along with his whole family in his car.Red alto.I felt little bit relax after seeing them. I asked him had you called the Ambulance. He answered "with in a minute it will be there". We all got in the house and saw my mom is crying and still rubbing my dadi's hand. My Aunty came close to dadi and gave a signal to my uncle that she is no more. My uncle shouted shut up he ran and put his fingers near her nostrils. He doesn't feel anything and seen towards aunty and shaked his head and started crying loudly. My mom still rubbing the hand and said "you all are liar, she can't leave us."

After hearing this I get down on my knees and start shouting in the loud voice

"she is making us fool, she had promised me last night for attending my marriage". My mom saw me saying this and started crying putting her hand on the forehead. The ambulance had come to the house and the driver came near to dadi and announced she is no more. I am praying to god just once wake her up, I will not allow her to leave me, please god wake her. Its 4:00 am in the morning every one in the colony had came to our house after hearing the sound of crying from the house. My uncle called me and asked today you have an exam. I answered while crying yes. He told me to get on the 1st floor to my room for study. I ignored once but still he forced me to go and said you will go for exam, we all are here to see everything. I got in my room and opened my book. But I didn't understand what I am doing and what should I do? The page which I had opened for study is all wet due to my tears.Everyone was crying. I closed my book and got in a corner of the room and start thinking of my dadi. As I am thinking of my dadi my tears are flowing from eyes. Its morning 8:00 am alarm rang I am still sitting in the corner with tears in my eyes, this time my father came to my room.

"dad I am not going anywhere by leaving you." I denied to go for exam.

"No son you have to go and give exam." My father hugged me and requested me to go.

He took out my college dress from the hanger and kept on the bed. He kissed me on my forehead and said me "best of luck".

I didn't discuss about this tragedy to anyone in college.I was continuously thinking of my dadi. Mukesh and Rahul were busy in studying physics at the stop. They just waved their hands towards me. I didn't respond towards them.

I am sitting in the examination room on the first bench and busy in analyzing the subject.My mind was blank.I tried to copy from the boy sitting in front of me. He said he will help me. As the bell rang for starting the exam, everyone start the exam as the hungry man start eating food. But I am sitting very relax and just thinking about the environment at my home. I seen towards the question paper, except filling my roll number, I didn't know anything in that. I tried to see at my back for cheating, but teacher came and caught me asked to sit at the last bench. I moved on to the last bench. I seen the student sitting in front of me is Rahul. Now I am sured that I am passed in physics. I told Rahul that I had not studied a single page of physics just show me 30 marks paper. He shaked his head to say ok. From the right side he starts showing me the copy. I start copying the exam as early as possible. I finished of 30 marks paper and get down my head on the bench. While putting my head down to the bench I am just thinking about the condition of home, how will I face the man at home? Every one at that time is crying at home and suppose if I didn't have tears in my eyes at that time, then what will they say to others that I am not feeling anything bad for my dadi. I am thinking that my all cousins and Aunties are present at home. Rahul shouted from front "just copy this numerical it is very short and of 5 marks."

I said "sorry Rahul I made fun of your dadi.Rahul today morning my dadi left me alone in this world."

"Ohh I am sorry Arnav. But now you concentrate on exam just copy this numerical."

I said leave it Rahul. And the time is over, the invigilator took answer sheet from me and Rahul.

We all got in the bus where everyone is discussing about the paper, but Rahul and Mukesh discussing about me. I am feeling guilty as they are seeing me with the eyes of sympathy. I entered in my room after facing the tough exam. My Brijesh uncle and Ravi Bhaiya are sitting on the sofa. I saw them and touched their feet. They asked me about the exam, I said it was fine. They asked me to get in to the room and changed the dress as fast as possible, we are going to finish the funeral system of dadi and we all are waiting for you. After hearing this eyes completely filled with tears. I changed my dress and came in the main hall. Every one is crying none of the person is sitting who has eyes not filled with tears.

At last finishing all the formalities, I thought that now I can concentrate on my studies for the remaining exams.But it dosent seem so. Some one was required to bring Amit uncle home. I took the initiative and took his number and called him and told him to wait at the reservation centre on Agra railway station. I got a call that Amit uncle had reached home along with Rakesh uncle and he forget to inform me.I went back home.the day ended, but still my mom and aunties are crying for her. It was previously heard from someone that at home till 13 days food will not be cooked,till then food will be ordered from outside.. My mom enquired about my exams and how was the schedule.One of my aunties called my mom. And without seeing towards me my mom got back in to the room. I went to my room. My room is the only place where no one is allowed.it's because of a community formed at my house who will decide everything for the next coming 13 days. This community is made up of the aged people. Those aged people will decide everything for the welfare of house.I was happy for this as I can study. I got in to my room for studies, but how its possible for me to study, last night my love leaved me alone, my loving grandmother left me in this world. I got in the corner and saw the watch it was 10:00 pm, today I am waiting for no call because Anadi told me, she will not call me anymore. And till now she had shifted to Noida with her complete family. There is no one to understand me and feel my pain. I am not getting for whom my tears are,for the one who loved me and left me, my dadi or for my love that I love the most. Complete night I had spended in that corner thinking about my dadi and when I feel alone I Miss Anadi. Next day again some rituals had started from morning and as I am a grand son so for me it's a must to take part.. Certain rules and regulation had been circulated among the house member. They are as follows——

1. They had announced in the family before 13 days no one will buy a single new thing from the market.
2. No one will try to cook some thing in the kitchen except tea because "we are Indians and we love tea".
3. No one will watch television; hear music etc in the house and their respective cars.

And the list goes on according to Hindu rituals.

The community had made a time table from morning to evening for the thirteen days. While going through the time table every one is realizing that we had lost some one and this was killing all the members of house every second of the thirteen days. Tomorrow is my last exam and today is the last day from the thirteen days. Everyone in the house is busy in doing work for the last day formalities. From morning itself the row of relatives are coming to our house for having food. Everyone is enjoying the food, but no one is realizing that the food which they are eating is made from tears and feelings for the one who left us forever. Hindu religions and rituals are always performing the complicated roles in front of science or in front of human being which didn't believe in all that. According to Veda's of India it was proved that after 84 lakhs, the life get human birth it means when you do good job in the last 84 lakhs life you will be present human birth in that. For a while lets make this theory, if we move to real life of human being we see 40 % of the Indians are not satisfied with his life, some is struggling his only one leg and begging on the Railway pull or a person with one hand is sitting in front of the temple, if they get a human life after doing their good job in last 84 lakhs life then why do they are facing all this.

Any how it's all going as usual and will continue till the last man on the earth.

After completing all the formalities of 13 days, mostly all the relatives had moved back to their houses. I am little bit worried for the last exam. As usual I didn't study anything for the exam; the answer sheet was in front of me.. The time had started to start answering in the copy. Today I am sitting on the third bench. Today I am missing Rahul. I saw at my back the one who is sitting had made his face that the subject is new to him, I told him to show something. He shook his head and said the paper is out of course. I asked from the student sitting in front of me, in a very slow voice "hey brother do you help me in getting 30 marks". He turned back without fear from the invigilator and told me please help me for 10 marks I didn't analyze the question paper. After seeing both the student tensed I felt little bit relax, I mumbled slowly I am not alone to get a back. I saw towards Rahul he too is upset with the paper. Till now I had not seen a single question of the question paper. I saw the first line of the paper it was written "Electro magnetic field theory" I remember the class when me, Rahul and Mukesh had decided to get back in this subject after seeing the formulae's written on the black board. I asked to the invigilator to go for toilet. He said come early. Rahul and Mukesh smiled after seeing me going as they know I am going to have some jack for passing the paper. I got in the toilet, the first thing I seen on the washbasin is "Electro magnetic field theory" notes. I put those notes in my socks and while I am going to class, some one called me from back "hey stop it". I turned back with a sweat on my forehead. It was peon, I felt little bit easy.

I came near to him and asked "you are the one who supplies tea to the Room Number 401."

He said "yes, first you take out the notes from your socks or I will shout".

I kept my right hand on his shoulder and asked his name.His name was Ajit.I talked with him for few minutes politely.It brought a smile on his face. I took out 150 Rupees from the pocket and gave him.

"Ajit, my half of the class is going to fail in this exam,you just have to celebrate your birthday today. In my room there is one invigilator. You just have to bring things to eat continuously for 1 hour. After he finishes one thing he will go to drink water at the water cooler at that time we will exchange the copy. Rest of the money will be yours. I smiled and got back to the room.". He was afraid but I manged to convince him.I came back in the room and was seeing outside to see Ajit. Ajit knocked the door and called the invigilator outside. I was scared whether Ajit is trying to cheat me. But he gave two samosas in the invigilators hand. After seeing him eating and concentrating him on the chutney, I took out the notes and started writing the answers. Everyone were begging to know one of the answer. I mumbled slowly to wait for 10 minutes. In 10 minutes I had completed my paper of 35 marks.The teacher went to drink water and I passed the notes towards Mukesh. After some time he brought some pastries.All this continued till the last 2 minutes of the exam. I got out of the room and thrown the notes in the toilet. Everyone is happy because today they had completed their 3rd semester but after exam I am missing my dadi. I reached home after facing the battle in college. Everyone had gone back to their respective home. My mom and dad are sitting on the dining table and having eyes filled with tears. After seeing them, I understood they are missing dadi. I didn't disturb them and moved to my room; my mom cleared her tears and told me, "Arnav take the food from kitchen". I said ok and got in to my room. I kept my bag on the table and took the glass of water from the table for drinking.while drinking I saw Anadi's ring in my finger.I was missing her a lot. I took out the ring from my finger, I kissed the ring twice and mumbled "why darling why you left me"?

I got on the roof to see whether, Anadi is there at home or not. But there are no clothes on the roof. The door is locked. I remember that she told with complete family they are shifting to Noida. I rubbed my eyes to clear the tears.Time went back and I remembered the first day when she told me to come on the roof. I didn't stop myself from crying after remembering the memories of Anadi. After completion of 2 hours my mom shouted from the ground floor "hey Arnav come and have food", I ignored and said I am not hungry. I opened my contact list and took out Anadi's number from it. I was scared whether she attends my call or not, she is married or not. If in case she is married her husband attends the call what will I say to him, who I am? I pushed the button dial on Anadi's number. I heard "the number you dialed is switched off please dial the number after some time". I am feeling myself not less then a beggar who always begs for Anadi. I don't know what should I do? I am hopeless and completely broken from inside. I fell down on bed and don't know when I went in to the dreams. My mom in the evening came to my room and woke me up. I was shocked when she suddenly came up with the topic of anadi.

"have you talked with Anadi after that day"?

First I was scared what answer should I give to this, if I say yes then she will tell me, we told you to don't talk, then why did you talked to her? If I say no, she will not believe me. She told me I know that she had gone to Noida with his whole family and now she is a married woman Mrs. Pratibha Sharma her neighbor had told me, while I am not sure.

"Will all this matter to you mom , she is married or not. She had not tried to think once of mine. How much I love her? You always took me as a joke; you always believed I am a kid. No mom my generation doesn't believe this word, that we are kids. I never told you to fix my marriage right now with her.I was ready to wait for her. But you didn't care of my feelings; you didn't have any respect towards my love, that's why generation always gets a last option of attempting bad things. The children need you in every joy, fun, pain and happiness.

"Arnav I know some places parents are wrong but every time they just want to see the welfare of their children."

"Yeah mom you are true and argument on the topic like this cant be over. I left my room and got down to the ground floor and wanted to be alone.

Love story rewinds.

In college from morning to evening I used to sit at the last bench lonely. Many a times Mukesh and Rahul tried to fresh up my mood, but I didn't change. I feel Anadi in my every heart beat. None of the moments is I am with myself. Every moment I feel my heart is beating just for Anadi. My heart always cries without tears.

In 4th semester b.tech, we have three common subjects in all the branches of our college. In which two have separate teachers and for one we have common teacher which is "Human Values". There are total four branches in my college. All are sitting in a common hall on the chairs. The concern teacher of the subject is teaching us and I am busy in playing Sudoku in my mobile at the last chair. The teacher had seen me twice, but he ignored me. A girl of Civil Engineering

Branch is sitting on my right hand; I had seen her first time in the college as the civil engineering students study in the different building. She mumbled slowly, why are you playing with mobile? I saw towards her, a perfect girl in all the sense of beauty. She is sitting by folding her legs on the chair. I didn't answer and again start playing. She again replied "Didn't you hear what I ask you?" I seen towards her and asked "why are you sitting like this?" She answered I feel good in this. Yes the last word good, I feel good, I answered. She smiled and seen on my mobile screen. I asked what you are thinking that I am seeing porn movies. No did I say this, she replied. The teacher Mr. Arnav Sharma and Miss Ahana Sharma you can continue your talking in the canteen, so please leave the class. Ahana seen towards me and said lets go. We both leaved the class. Ahana told me sorry Arnav because of me; you lost your one attendance. I told her its ok and start moving towards the canteen. She shouted "hey Arnav can I join you in the canteen". Yes why not? I said. Can I see your highest score in Sudoku? Before completing her sentence she took my mobile from hand. Hey it's a nice one, Ahana said. Thanks. I replied. So, Ahana where do you live? She answered I live in Ram Nagar Colony Agra, with my family. And you Arnav, she asked. I live in Agra.

Ahana what do you want to eat? I asked. No Arnav just before this lecture I had finished my lunch. Ok then we would have a coffee. I said. She said, ok. I ordered two cups of coffee at the canteen counter and paid the amount of coffee. Ahana shouted hey Arnav I will pay for that, take your money back. I said its ok. She came to the counter and given the total amount. I said, no the better way is, we should share the amount. She said, yuppie, idea is good.

We had shared the amount, till then the cups of coffee are ready. We get back to the chairs. Ahana seen towards me and asked "is it my last cup of coffee with you"? I stared towards her and asked what do you mean by this? She said I want to be your friend, if you don't mind. I smiled and said we are friends now. She smiled and said cheers to our friendship with the cups of coffee. She asked to me "did my friend is on face book or not"? I said yes. We had completed our coffee and till then the class is over, surprisingly Mukesh had came near me and said "hey after how many days you have a smile on your face and it's because of a girl, we didn't matter to our friend hmm". Ahana hear the last sentence spoke by Mukesh and given a smile. Ahana said "ok Arnav my friends are waiting for me, I am going". I said ok bye. She wants to say many things to me, but because of Mukesh she can't say bye in better manner. "Hey what are you talking to her, from so much long time" Mukesh asked. I said nothing brother, we are just giving introduction to each other. We left the canteen and move on to the college gate for bus. I am searching for Ahana, where is she? But I didn't see her. In the evening at home I had opened my account on face book, as usual I do in the evening for an hour. I checked my friend request it was one request pending. After seeing one friend request, a voice came inside from me "it was definitely from Ahana" and the voice are true, it was really from Ahana. I confirmed the friend request. At home page I had seen the green indication that Ahana is online. I opened the chat box and send a message "hey how was the coffee?" she answered it was not chocolaty then the new friend. Ohh really, I replied. "Hey Arnav I want to ask one thing"? She said. And what's that? At the time we are leaving, your friend is saying that, "you had laughed after so much time" what this mean? Ohh that one, it means I had laughed after so much time, I replied. Is it true, she asked? Yes, it is true. Ahana asked me the reason behind this. I told her, it was a long story. If I start write on face book, you can publish it as a novel. I don't know anything, I want to know everything about you, she said. Ok I will narrate my story in the next "Human Value" lecture tomorrow. She said ok. I gave him the excuse and leave the face book. After switching off the computer, I am thinking about the Ahana not about Anadi. I feel that she is the one who can help me in forgetting Anadi. I discovered many dreams with Ahana, I will be her best friend, and I will share every secret with Ahana and the long list of dreams. Next day in college, I am waiting for the last lecture of my favorite subject "Human Value". At last my waiting gets over and the time for lecture had come. The first man inside the common hall was me to choose the perfect place, from where no one can disturb me and Ahana, whether he was teacher or any college mate. And at last in the corner I saved to chairs, one for me and other for my new friend Ahana. Rahul came near me and sit on the chair which I had saved for Ahana. I am hesitating to say Rahul, change the seat. But my friend Mukesh, the friend of my first peck of wine had shown his true friend ship. Mukesh called Rahul for some notes of "Human values". Rahul asked me, can I go and sit with Mukesh he is calling me. I said yes why not Rahul, go and have fun in lecture. He left the chair; my eyes are on the white color wooden gate from where all students are coming. The teacher had entered in the hall. All the chairs are filled with the students, only the chair parallel to me whom I had saved for Ahana was empty. The teacher had started the lecture but Ahana didn't come to hall. I am feeling bad; I am seeing dreams and she had destroyed all of them. My mobile vibrate once, it was a message. I opened it. The message from unknown number, I opened the inbox it was written "hey I am waiting for you in canteen, come soon" and in last of the message it was written "from your new friend". I feel little bit relax and start planning to go out of the class. Suddenly in between the lecture I had taken out my water bottle and stored some of the water in my mouth and start running towards the window, which is in parallel with the teacher's podium. I peaked out the whole water from my mouth and said "sir it was vomit can I go to toilet please" yes hurry up, do you want help of some one. He asked. No sir, I don't want and by saying this I ran from the class as the natural actor. And my toilet was at canteen. Before 200 meters I seen someone is sitting in the canteen and it was girl. I opened my inbox and called on the same number. Hello, I said. Ahana said, yes its mine number come to the canteen. Hey from where you get my number? I asked on phone itself. I got it on face book. She answered and drops the call. I reach canteen and offer my hand in front her to shake, she accept and shaked her hand. The first question she asked me is, "where are you till now"? I am in the class, as I said you on face book, I said. But you had told me to narrate your story, she asked. Yes I said but in the class, I had also saved a chair after having so much trouble in the corner for you in the hall. Ohh so sweet, but I thought you had told for the canteen, she said. Had you order some thing Ahana? No I didn't, she said. We order two burger and some fries. As usual we had shared the amount. Hey Arnav please tell me the reason for what you had left smiling, Ahana asked. Hey its nothing like that, I just love to live alone. I said. Mr. Arnav Sharma don't make me fool just narrate your story, I am dieing to hear that, I think the story is concern with your girlfriend, hmm. Ahana said. Yes you are right, I answered. Ohh it's so nice, so who's she and what's her name? She asked. Her name is Anadi, Anadi Gupta. Hey it's an awesome name. Ahana said. Yes it is and from the beginning of my love to the end of my love, I narrate her complete story. Ohh so sorry Arnav I don't ever think, that you are facing that much of difficulties now a days I will never force you to speak all this about this. No Ahana its ok, I told you all this because I feel my new friend will help me forgetting all this. So I am correct or not. I asked. Yes you are Arnav; I will try my level best.

Thanks Ahana, it is enough for me to hear the last word from you that you are with me. So my new friend did not have any boy friend. Arnav after meeting to you in two days I am feeling that, I know you from the decades. She said. Hey don't turn topic, I want to no about you. I said. Yes I have one boy friend last year, she said. Ohh that's great, I said. What the fuck great? He is a bloody boy on the name of love. He made me fool by saying that he loves me and I love him by true feelings. In the last he tried to get in physical touch with me. When I ignored him to do that in a hotel. Next day he calls me in the morning at the time of break fast I am eating Maggie. I seen my phone is ringing, the number is from him. I received the call and his last words are "don't ever try to call me, I want a break up from you" and my eyes filled with the ocean's. And from that day I decided not to have "what". She stopped in between saying all this. I said "what" means boy friend. No the "Maggie". Ohh shut up please don't give a joke. No really I hate Maggie and from that day I didn't tasted the Maggie, complete one year is going to be over. I said great epic. After hearing her story all her story I want to say her "lol". But I want to understand her emotions and respect her feelings. I said don't worry Ahana you will definitely get some one better then that. She said, yes I am waiting for that. We both are hearing some sound, she checked out her watch and said "the class is over; I don't want to know my friends that I am with you". I said ok, bye. And we both move to our bus. After reaching home I checked out my messages on face book, but there is no message from Ahana. After shutting down the system, my phone starts vibrating in my pocket. I checked out it was from Ahana. I received the phone and she said to me "hey Arnav I am missing you", I said, I am too missing you my new friend. Arnav you are the only one with whom I had discussed, so much closely about my past love. I want you to be with me always. Yes definitely I will try my level best. I disconnect the phone after saying the last line. In the night about 1:00 am, I am thinking about Anadi, is she happy with her new family. Is her husband cooperative with her or not. Will she misses me or not? I have many questions to ask, but there is no one present to hear me. And the phone starts ringing. I am scared at this time "who is there"? I picked my phone from the table and seen it was from Ahana. I smiled and attend the call. She said in the beginning, "Hey Arnav, I am missing you too much can't forget you for a single second". I tried to make her fool, "hey who's that at this time"? I said this in heavier voice. Ahana mumbled in a scary voice "who are you"? I am Arnav dad. After hearing this she disconnect the phone. I called her back she didn't attend the call, continuously I had ringed three times but she didn't respond. I messaged her "hey don't worry my new friend, I am Arnav not Arnav dad". After receiving the message she called me and first words are "I will kill you Arnav". I said, how can you kill; you said to my dad that you are missing me. Arnav please don't make my fun. Please try to understand, I had not leaved you for a single second in my heart. Ahana said. I tried to ignore her; I am feeling that she is getting in love with me. Ok then good night Ahana. She shouted, Arnav I am serious with you and you are ignoring me. Ok-ok I am sorry, what are you saying? I asked. Arnav I want to meet you. She said. But tomorrow is Sunday, we will meet on Monday now can I sleep please Ahana. I said. Hey not on Monday, just now she said in bold voice. Ahana please it's not time for a joke the clock showing 1:15 am. Arnav I am not joking, please give me your address I am coming. Ahana are you mad, how's it possible? I shouted. Arnav please try to understand, only once from the out of your house, I will see you and come back to my home. Ahana I don't understand what are you saying, you are a girl and it's dangerous to out at this time in the city? I don't care, she said. And your parents, I asked. I have a separate room in my house and it will open at the morning after 8:00 am. No I will not allow you to come out of your house at this time. But I want to see you Arnav just now. She said. Can't you wait for 6:00 am I will come to your house. I said. I want to see you just now and then what does it mean for me to come in the morning? She said. Ahana you are really very difficult, give me some time to think. Ok fine, Ahana said. I disconnect the phone and planned everything to meet Ahana as she is forcing me; if she came to house it might some tragedy in the route. I send a message to her "what's your address?" in the next message she replied with her address. After getting the address, one thing I want is bike and if I go on my bike, my parents will catch me. I called Mukesh as he is living on rent and have a personal bike, hey Mukesh sorry for disturbing you but I want your bike till morning. He asked for what "I explained him everything"; Mukesh agreed and called me to came at his house for bike. I get out of the house through the water pipe as first time in life I know the second use of water pipe. It was 5 minute distance from my house to Mukesh house; I ran and reached to Mukesh house. He is standing outside with the bike. He said me please take care of your self. I kicked the bike and said thanks while putting the first gear. After changing the first gear to second gear, I have one thing in my mind "why I am doing this?" and the answer I got is "to see happiness on my friends face". And I changed to top gear for smooth running of the bike. I reached the address that was given by the Ahana, I seen at the second floor of the house "a girl is standing on the balcony, but that's not Ahana" I move the bike from the front of her house. My mobile is vibrating it was from Ahana, I received the call. Hey thank you baby to come for me. "Where are you?" I asked. See back the girl you had seen had changed in to me. I seen back Ahana is waving her hand. I asked who that girl is. She was my sister, she said. Ok, now can I go back to home? I asked. She said, are you mad just park your bike at the corner of the road and jump the boundary to get on the window shed I am opening it come inside to my room. Ahana if some one caught me you will be fired. Don't worries do what I am saying? I do the complete process what she is indicating me? And finally I reach to her room. I sit on her bad and taken some breathe of relax. She came close to me and said "from last evening after canteen, I am missing you to much". Ahana I am feeling scary after seeing your behavior. She said don't worry I will not rape you, but can I hug you darling. In her eyes I can easily see the love for me, but I can't say no to her. Because I am the one who is enjoying all this after Ahana. She came close to me and given me a smooched. She left me after kissing on my face after 2 minutes. We both are sleeping on the bad in parallel to each other and breathing fast. Ahana told in her vibrating voice I love you Arnav. I didn't answer of her. She again told me "Arnav I love you". Ahana sorry but I love Anadi. She waked up and asked then what the hell you are doing her. It's because you love me not that girl Anadi. No Ahana I had came here just for you. What rubbish no one can do this for a friend. But I do Ahana. I said. I saw towards the clock of Timex showing 4:00 am of the morning. I told Ahana "just now I have to go, my father will wake up at 5:00 am for morning walk and before that I have to reach house. I waked up from the bad, I seen Ahana is crying, hey Ahana why you are crying, you know this already, that I love Anadi. But Arnav I love you can't see you thinking and talking of other girl. Ahana please try to understand me, I am always your friend but I can't love you and if you feel bad for the smooch then sorry for that. Arnav don't be and thanks for coming. She hugged me after saying the last word. I mumbled please say the last word and hugged me again. But the next word he said is bye. Again after the same process by which I had came to the room, I get back to my room. Its 4:45 am in the morning. After 15 minutes my father waked up for his marathon, he had come on leave for ten days. I tried to sleep but my mobile again start vibrating and it's again from Ahana. I received the call "hey sweetheart had you reached home safely". Yes, but please Ahana at this time I want to sleep. I replied. Arnav cant you talk to me for 5 minutes. Ok start "what do you want to say"? I said. Arnav I want to spend my every moment with you. Ohh really Ahana, I said. Arnav I am in love please try to understand baby. Ahana do you know how much I love Anadi "the words you are using for me, I am missing Anadi too much", then say me how can I love you, when my heart always beats for Anadi. But she is now a married girl and you have to forget her. She said. Ahana I know that you are right but I don't know why my heart always says, she is still waiting for me somewhere. What the fuck is your heart feels? If there is something like that she will call you, its so much time had passed away. She said. I don't know Ahana. I said. Then who knows about you, she replied. I am disconnecting the phone call you later. I said and disconnect the phone. After disconnecting the phone I am feeling the pain in Ahana's heart for me. I am depressed, what should I do know at this stage? One side I have a love who is not with me and the other side the girl who loves me but I didn't feel anything for her. Its 8:00am in the morning, last night I had not slept for a single minute. My mom called me for the break fast from the ground floor. I said no for that. I had gone for a sleep, a about 5:00 pm in evening I waked up. I saw my phone its 92 missed call and 51 messages. I am shocked what the fuck phone is showing, it might some software problem in mobile. But when I checked out the miss call it was from Ahana and all the messages from Ahana. In the entire messages only one thing is written "miss you darling too much please call me once". I called her after seeing the messages. Thanks darling for call me back. She said. Ahana listen one thing you love me, it's very good and continue your love with me but only in heart don't show me. If you want to be me then only with a relation of a good friend, other you are good on your way and I am good on my way. Arnav I love you and how can I ignore this thing, when I live with you. Ahana replied. But why don't you understand I don't feel anything for you. I said.

Ok then we will be with each other as a good friend. She said. Yes it will be fine and please never force me to say this entire thing again in life, I feel embarrassed. I said. Ahana agreed on all my condition to live as a true friend

Not as a lovers. From next day in college we mostly bunk the lecture of "Human Values" and sit in the canteen compound. Many a times we bunked the complete day of college and gone to see the movies in Multiplex. My life is going like a man who has a chocolate in front of him to eat but I don't want to eat that. Ahana many a times tried to say her feelings about love, but every time I ignored her. She had started calling me daily in night and I enjoyed talking with her. I share everything with her. But mostly my talking starts with Anadi and end with Anadi. Many a times Ahana got depressed with me about talking of Anadi and she disconnect the phone, then I have to complete the formalities of pleading and saying sorry to her. Day after tomorrow my external exams are going to be start of 4th semester. Ahana called me before starting of the exam and said me best of luck for the exam. I am nervous for the exam; as usual I had come to give exam on the basis of cheating. I entered the room and Ahana is sitting the room, I checked out the list of sitting arrangement it was fourth row third column. I moved to search for my seat and surprisingly it was with Ahana. When I get sit on the bench with Ahana she touched my feet with his feet. I seen towards her and said please Ahana I am nervous don't do this. She told, ohh my baby is nervous, don't worry I will help you in the exam. I laughed and said you get time after messages and calls. She has three subjects similar with my branch. I said Ahana don't worry for three I will help you and for the remaining subject "I am sorry". She said ohh really sweet heart thank you so much, she said. The invigilators shouted don't talk. I stopped talking and moved my head in front. Today we both have different subject. After getting the question paper, Ahana start writing his answer sheet "I mumbled what are you writing, story me and you" Ahana said do your paper Arnav please other wise you will fail. I seen question paper only two answers I know in the whole question paper. I completed the answers in 5 minutes and head down on the bench facing towards Ahana. She seen me and again hit me with his feet. I shouted oouuuch, the invigilators seen and asked what happen. Sir mosquito, everyone in the room laughed on me including Ahana. I mumbled mosquito is female very smart and big in size. She mumbled stop it why are you not doing the work. I mumbled how I can do this time. I said. What do you mean? She asked. First let them the front bencher finish the work then I will exchange the copy. Are you mad? She asked. You are mad if I don't do this then I will failed, only two answers I know in the whole question papers. She stared towards me and starts doing her work. After one hour I asked to my front bencher for the copy, he given his copy from inside the bench. I start copying from that. Ahana seen me doing this and said once we reach home, I will kill you Arnav. In the next hour I had given back the copy of front bencher and take the copy from my back bencher who always starts his paper from last, this is how I completed my question paper. The time is over and I given back the copy to concern one. We moved from the examination room. I met with a boy who is Ahana's classmate who is sitting behind my bench, he stopped me and said "hey Arnav please help me in doing cheating from Ahana's copy" I asked are you mad she is a fool how can she help you, if you copy from her copy then definitely you will be fail in the exam. The boys told me are you mad she stands first in our branch. I am shocked and didn't given any answer about him move back to home. I reached home and called Ahana I asked "at what position do you stand in class"? She told, last time I stand first in class. I shouted why you don't tell me this in the beginning. What's there to tell in this? She replied. Yes there is a thing to tell. I said. I am sorry Arnav I don't mean this thing to tell you, for me in front of you doesn't matter all this. I am disconnecting the phone; I have to study for tomorrow's exam. I said. Ohh really, my awesome cheater. She said. For you it's an easier task to give exam as you are topper, not for me. Ok Arnav I will not disturb you, do your preparation and she disconnect the phone. Till the next day I had not read a single word for the exam, just busy in thinking about Ahana that she is good in studies but still she don't have any feeling of ego in her. She is so polite, clam and mannered person in front of everyone. In the morning, before entering in the room I seen Ahana is sitting or not and she is sitting. I entered the room and sit on the bench. I asked Ahana which exam you have, she said "Industrial Psychology". "Hey me to have this exam" so how's your preparation Ahana. Its fine and yours Arnav. It's really fantastic; I had read all four units. I answered. But the total number of units is five. She asked. I had read one unit before these exams. I answered. Ohh that's good. She said. I said so Miss Topper, "wish you all the best" and if you want help from me in between the exam, please don't hesitate. Arnav you so much well prepared for this exam, she said. Yes Ahana. And the invigilators start distributing the question papers. We all received the question paper, I start writing the question on the answer sheet before starting Ahana to do her exam. Till one hour I am busy in writing question on the answer sheet, so that she thinks that I am writing the answer. Ahana put her pen on the bench and said I had finished my paper, I seen towards her and said I had too finished my exam. She smiled and mumbled I am really very happy for you that you became so serious for studies. She asked me had you written question number 5 in the answer sheet. I said yes. She asked me please show me, I had some doubt in that. And know I am fired. I turned my page and at every page it was only questions are written, I shown her the question number 5. What the fuck is this Arnav? She asked. You asked for question number 5 not for answer of question number 5 and here it is question number 5. I said. Arnav are you mad, it means you had not studied anything? Start copying from my copying for passing marks, Ahana said. Sorry Ahana it's about my prestige, I can't copy from my girlfriends copy. After saying this I moved for toilet. I had come back to class after 15 minutes. I seen Ahana is writing something, I smiled and mumbled to Ahana "what are you writing when you had finished your exam?" Just shut your mouth and don't disturb me, if you don't want to do your exam, its fine but please don't disturb me. Ahana said. I put my head down on the bench and gone for a sleep. I mumbled Ahana wake me up before five minutes of the exam to over. Ahana stared towards me and said you are ridiculous. I said thank you baby. Ahana waked me up, hey stupid wake up its 5 minutes remaining take your copy and give mine. I don't have your copy, I said. The copy in front of you is mine, I exchanged while you had gone to toilet. Hey Ahana it mans you had cheated all my answers from my copy, you are so bad. What the fuck you had written in your answer sheet, so that I will cheat from that. Yes you are correct then what you are doing with my copy, I asked. I had completed your copy with all the answers. I exchanged the copy and seen, she had written all the answers. I said thank you Ahana. It's ok Arnav I have to talk with you after exam in the matter of your bloody prestige. In the evening I am watching movies on the computer my phone rings, I seen it's from Ahana; I received and said what are you doing Mr. Prestige man. Nothing more I am just studying for tomorrow's exam. I said. As you had done yesterday. She said. I laughed and said actually I am watching movies. I said. I know you Mr. Arnav very well. She replied. I had planned something for tomorrow's exam. We both have same exam tomorrow and you will finish your exam within an hour and after that you feel bore in the examination room. So what you had planned, Mr. Arnav. I had that you will solve my question and do time pass. Ohh thank you Arnav you are so kind hearted, you are always concern about me. She said. Its ok Ahana don't say thanks to me, you are my friend. And next day according to my plan everything is going on I had buyed some of the ground nuts and putted some of them in the pocket, while Ahana is doing my work I am eating groundnuts and after every question I give her one ground nut as a prize.

We had finished our exams and have again 30 days holidays as a summer vacation. In holidays I had not gone any where else then from my home. My morning start with Ahana's call night and night end with Ahana's call. Whole day I just busy with Ahana sometimes on face book while chatting and playing games online and rest on mobile. We met 6 days from 10 days with this ratio I spent all my holidays.

Tomorrow is my first day of 5th semester. I am forgetting Anadi day by day; I start feeling that I love Ahana more then Anadi. Ahana is a good then Anadi. Ahana understands my feelings, cares and give me respect with all her regards. She never tries to compare her with Anadi, in every field whether it was about smartness or in studies. Almost half of the semester is going to over. Today my result has come of 4th semester, I got 54 % in that, much more then I thought. Ahana and I use to talk late in the night daily. As usual in the night we are talking to each other on phone. Ahana told me "hey Arnav do you know I write poems and I had also write some lines for you". Ohh really, so start singing. I said. Now Arnav, she asked. Yes just now, I am really dieing to hear those lines which you had written for me. I said. Ok but I have condition don't laugh on me and comment after I finish. She said. Ok done, I said.

Respected and my dear love Arnav for you I am going to say few lines, I hope you will try to understand my feelings by these lines.

Tumhare bina jeene ki sochu to tham jaati hai saanse or jhalakte h aansu…

Karti hu Mei pyar tumse par kaise kahu ye baat tumse……

Sath bitaya har pal - har lamha, jinda rakhti hun is dil Mei sirf tumse…..

Tumhare bina jeene ki sochu to tham jaati hai saanse or jhalakte h aansu…

WO ehsaas hi ajab hota h jo hota h tumhare sath hone se…..

Kaise nikalu unhe apne man se…..

Janti hu hona alag h ek din humko, par jaane kyu darti hu uss din se….

Mile tumhe saari khusiya jindagi Mei, yahi dua h rab se…

Tumhare bina jeene ki sochu to tham jaati hai saanse or jhalakte h aansu…

Shukriya…..apki apni Ahana…

So how's that Arnav, she asked after finishing the poem. I am just feeling bad for her that she loved the one who is not capable of her. "Hey Arnav I am sorry for irritating you by this stupid poem" she said. Wow…No Ahana it's really very good or I can say it's a fantastic fabulous from you. I said. Still I have tears in my eyes for her. Ahana I want to say something, I am feeling that I am in love with you. But every time when I think about love with you, I don't know why I feel Anadi is waiting for me. And if one day Anadi came and asked to me "do you love me or some one else" and at that moment what should I answer. Arnav why don't you understand that now she is a married woman, if she has to come she will already come, its almost 8 months are over. I think you are right Ahana; I should forget her and restart my life from the new beginning. I said.

My exams of 5th semester are going start from tomorrow and I had stopped disturbing Ahana from 10 days before. We used to talk only 15-20 minutes in a day. I promised her to study well for exam, but as usual I am just busy doing something else than that of study. This time my luck doesn't work and Ahana is in different class and I am sitting on the first bench of the examination hall. I used answer every question in the exam whether I am sure about that answer or not. Any how I had given my exams of 5th semester. My 10 days leave of winter vacation are going on. I am much close to Ahana. But till now I had not touched her after the first day of smooch kiss given by her. We are talking in the night on phone; suddenly Ahana told me, "If I ask you to kiss me, will you kiss me Arnav". Yes off course why not? I said. If I say to open my clothes will you do it for me? She asked. Yes definitely, but first tell me are you seeing the porn movie just now? I said. Ohh shut up Arnav just answer me what I am asking to you. She shouted. Ok continue sweetheart. Arnav if I say you to touch my breast with your hand will you do it for me. She said in very slow voice as she is feeling me with her. Yes darling I said. If I say to nude me, will you do it for me? She said. I am confirmed that she wants me to with her tonight; still I said why you are asking to me? Arnav I want to feel my love, I want to hear your breathe from closest to the power of infinity, don't you want you to feel me. She said. Yes darling, I am curious to see you nude darling. Arnav cant you come to my home. She asked. When darling? I asked. She said just now. Its 12:05 am and I will be there at your room till 12:30 am. She said ok sweetheart I am waiting. I called Mukesh again for the bike, he agreed on giving me bike. I get down trough the water pipe from my home and ran towards Mukesh house. I reached at his house and as usual he had played a best friends role in my life by filling the petrol tank full. I kicked the bike and reached to Ahana's house she is waiting for me at the balcony of the back of house. I parked the bike below the same tree at the corner of the road. After jumping from the boundary I get in to the beautiful window of the world. Ahana where's your parents and sister. My mom and sister are sleeping in the bedroom at ground floor and father is out of station for some office work. So my darling is alone alone at this floor. I smiled after saying the last precious sentence. I am sitting on the bed and Ahana is sitting on the chair she take water bottle from the "whirlpool" fridge of red color having rust in the foot of it. after taking water bottle, I said don't you think at this time instead of drinking cold water I should drink hot milk as we are going to have our golden night. Ya off course, I call my mom she will give you from the kitchen, she smiled. I said then leave it. We should not disturb your mom. She switched off the main light and switched on the night lamp. She is standing near that rusted fridge and putting the water bottle inside it. She had weared red color salwar and kurta; she has not putted duppata on her. I came near him and hugged her from the back. She didn't say anything to me picked my hand to her stomach. I turned her face towards me and kissed me on my lips, her breast is touching my chest. She is much closer to me and continuously kissing on my eyes then forehead then my cheek. She opened my shirt and kissed on the chest. I pulled towards me and hugged her. From the back I am busy in opening her "kurta" and make her little far from me and opened her "salwar". She is complete nude standing in front of me. I fell her down on the bed of her room. I came near her and get sleep over her. I am kissing on her breast, her stomach and on her thy's. She opened my jeans pant and start rubbing her lips near thy's. We both are nude at this moment and I seen towards her eyes, they are closed. After seeing her face with closed eyes, I just remember the Anadi's face. After having her face I removed my hand from her back. She opened her eyes and seen that my eyes are filled with tears. She shouted, "hey Arnav what happen? She leaved me on the bed and get sitted on my parallel. I didn't answer anything of her last question. She again shouted "Arnav I am asking something, if you don't want to do this we will stop this". I am sorry Ahana. In a very slow and deep voice having tears in my eyes. For what, till now we both are virgin and you are not raping me. Ahana I am not joking. Then what the fuck you are doing at this time in this condition having girl nude in front of you and you are crying. Ahana I am missing Anadi, I love her and can't do all this except her. After hearing this Ahana feel tears in her eyes. I said, I am sorry Ahana, I am feeling that I love you, but really I don't ever mean to hurt to you. Every time my emotions for you are always true never want you to do fake with you. I said. Don't say anything else Arnav I know that you had never make me fool. You are right at your stage, I am wrong. I always think, I will love you that much, that one day you will forget Anadi. But it's really impossible. Anadi is very lucky girl, that you love her so much. I pray to god that you will get her. Thank you Ahana and I am really very sorry for that. I said. Don't be Arnav, we are still good friends and I hope we will sit together in the 6th semester external exams, this time we have 2 common subject's. Ohh Ahana my darling, I will never forget you darling. Hey don't think that I leaved you, I will disturb you always as a good friend. She said. From you Ahana I always want to get disturb. I said. I weared all my clothes and said Ahana to take care. I jumped from the window and then from the boundary. I am giving ignition to my bike and

I seen towards the house. Ahana had put the curtain on the window and from the corner she is waving her hand. Her eyes are full of tears. She is looking like a girl for whom everything is been finished.

Game rewind by Destiny

My 6th semester had started in college. I am feeling very lonely without Ahana, as she talks only 30 minutes in a week. I didn't understand why I left Ahana? I know very well that Anadi is a married woman. I tried to contact many times with Anadi, but I didn't found any clue about her. I always used to go in Vidhyut Nagar Colony to talk with Manish (the boy with whom I used to play cricket in that colony) about akash as I had not discussed with him about my love. Every month I used to go and ask him but he always ignored me. One day again I had gone to meet him. We both are sitting on the one and only bench in park. I thought of saying everything to him today about my love.

I asked, "Manish do you remember the girl Anadi, Akash's sister."

" Yes I remember, for her marriage Akash family had moved to

Noida. My mom says that girl have some relation with a boy in Agra. She wants to marry that boy, but her parents didn't agree with her."

" Manish do you know that boy.That boy is me, with whom she wants to marry."

" Ohh stop it Arnav." He said.

"Manish I am serious." I said.

"Wow, you are that lucky guy.".

"What the fuck lucky guy, she had leaft me and married with some one else."

"Do you know what she had done?" He asked.

"Yes she had faked me, nothing else than that.".

"Shut up Arnav, do you know she is been forced by her parents to do that. After forcing so much she is agreed to marry with that man. On the marriage night she stood in front of all the relatives and said I love some one else. If I marry it will be that boy, otherwise I will do suicide. The boy's family had rejected Anadi and taken back the Barat.After seeing all this Anadi's family told Anadi to leave them for ever, they don't want to continue any relation with her."

I was a fool.She still loves me. I wished I could have talked with Manish earlier.Manish didn't knew any further details about where she lived and where is she right now.Not even his mom as marriage was in some hall nearby.

"do you have that marriage card?Please Manish, go and search it." I said. "Don't worry Arnav; I am going to search that."

I am sitting on the bench from where my love story had started and hope it will restart. I am sitting on the bench and seeing towards the house no. 11. I am praying to the god just once give me a chance.Anadi this time I will fight with every one. That marriage card is my last option to search Anadi. I am mumbling "please Anadi come back once I will never let you go".

I saw Manish is coming towards the bench. I am seeing towards his hands, as he finds out the card or not. But unfortunately he was empty handed. He came near me and sits on the bench.He had kept the card in his pocket.He picked out the card from his pocket, my eyes got little bit relax after seeing the name of Anadi on the card. I turned the page three addresses are written on that. One of the boy second of Anadi and the last one of the marriage hall. I saw the middle one that was of Anadi. I put that card inside my jeans. "Thank you Manish for this card." I said.

"Its ok Arnav but what will you do next?" He asked.

"First I have to find her. I said. he hugged me, while going out of the park. I got back to home and first dialed all the numbers written on the card, but all the numbers are switched off.

House number 45, M.R.D.A. Colony, Noida.

Without thinking anything else then Anadi, I just decided to go

Anadi house in Noida. Now I have to plan something to say lie to mom. I called mom to my room and said, "Hey mom just now I got the news from Mukesh, that tomorrow our college is going for an industrial visit for two days in Noida. And tomorrow I have to deposit 1000 Rupees in college. Tomorrow itself they will submit the money and then we will move to Noida."

Next day in the morning, my mom had prepared a lunch box and a tourist bag with two dresses. I picked my bag and instead of going to college bus stand, I move to ISBT Agra. From there I picked the bus to Delhi. I am going to Delhi first time. From Delhi, it was one hour run as I heard. The ticket was Rs. 140. I have to manage everything with in 1000 Rupees. After a long run of 4.5 hour, I reached Delhi. The bus had dropped me to Kale khan bus stand in Delhi. I took out that card for address and startede asking the address from the bus driver, tourist, the brij pana wala. At last an auto driver had came to me and said "hey brother I am seeing you from so much time that you are trying to ask something, tell me where do you want to go". I gave him a sweet smile and mumbled still there are good persons in this world, always ready to help some one. I shown him the address and asked "how to reach this"?

"Ohh M.R.D.A. Colony, Noida. From here you will not get any bus or auto it was 50 km from here.I can drop you till there but it will charge Rs.400." "what the fuck, are you mad Rs 400?" I said.

"Ok then take care of your self, no value of goodwill." I thought twice and in front of me I am seeing only one face and that is of Anadi. I shouted "hey stop it, do some concession man it was really too much. I said. He said for you I will charge Rs. 350 but not less then this. I said ok lets go. After complete one hour I reached that M.R.D.A. Colony. I gave the money to auto driver and got in the colony. I asked the house number 45 from the guard. He told me it's on the right hand in front of Mandir. I reached the house number 45 and knocked the door. I am praying let Anadi open the door. But it was a 35 year lady opened the gate and I am sure she was not Anadi. She asked who are you, with whom you want to meet. I said can I meet Akash. Who akash, I live here alone? And after saying the last word she shut the door on my face...the only words I remembered is DIL WALO KI DILLI. I asked the guard sitting on the gate about the Anadi. He didnt know. I shown him the card, he answered this card was too long. Then I asked the second address of that boy Mr. Arpit Gupta, lecturer in Akashdeep Engineering College, Noida. I asked the address of that college from that guard. He told me to take an auto from out side the college it was 1 hour run from here. I mumbled again Rs. 350. I asked how much it will charge. He answered it was about 100 Rupees. I said thank god I saved Rs. 250. I seen the watch it was 4:00 pm in the evening. I thought generally the college will open till 5:00 pm. I picked the auto and asked him to go that college, this time the auto driver agreed on 100 Rs. I am saying him to drive fast other wise the college will be closed. But the big city showed his face, the big jams after every 5 minute run. I reached the college at 6:00 pm, the gate was closed. I leaved the auto and asked the guard of the college about the teacher standing on the gate. They told there are 100 teachers in this campus and every month many of them change their college and many of them come new, so how its possible to remember the name of the lecture. I saw the address of his home. 25, new hospital road Noida, I asked the same auto driver standing near the college gate. He asked 300 Rs for that. I seen the total amount it was Rs. 400 left. I said lets go. I am sitting in the auto and a fire is burning inside my stomach. Then I remember I had not eaten the food. I checked out my lunch that mom had putted in the bag, it smelled. I thrown out of the auto and just thinking this was my last attempt after that there is no address remaining to search her. I reached the house. I had given the money to auto driver only 1 note of 100 Rupees is remaining. I knocked the door and a boy of age about 30 yr had opened the door, I said if I am not wrong you are Arpit. He said yes, I am Arpit. I told him that I had come from Agra and given him the introduction. After hearing about me, he pushed me out of the gate and said because of you, me and my family is been insulted in front of society get lost from here. He closed the door.

I called "please Mr.Arpit, I want to talk you just for a minute.'

I am knocking the door continuously; again he opened the door and slapped me on the face. I fell down on the ground and he shouted go from here other wise I will call police. I moved out of the house.I saw my watch it was 8:00 pm, I am moving on the road and saw Arpits neighbor house, the name plate was of Mr. S.K. Gupta. I remembered that Arpit is her maasi's neighbor. Again a ray of light is been fired in my heart. I knocked the door, this time before giving my complete introduction I remembered the slap given by Arpit. A lady of age 50 year had opened the door; I said "namaste" auntiji. She smiled and said namaste beta, who are you? I said auntiji I am Akash's friend from Agra.

"Ohh you came from Agra, you coame on a very good time akash came to our house yesterday itself for his holidays." She called me inside and shouted Akash come on beta see your friend come from Agra.

I saw Akash is coming from the stairs. He saw me and shouted "Arnav, why did you come here, just get lost from here or I call the police?"

Maasi shouted, "what happened beta?"

Akash answered" nothing maasi I will see that bustard."

I said "please akash just try to understand me, just listen once I will go forever from here, I want to talk you for a minute." He picked my collar and said "first get out of the house". He pushed me outside the house.

I shouted “please Arnav just tell me where is Anadi?”

He said we have no relation with that bitch and kicked me on my nose and my bag fell down on the ground. I came near him and asked; just tell me where she is akash please. He said on the day of marriage, we thrown her out of the house and after that we had not tried to contact that bitch, its better that bitch come in front of any truck. I picked his collar and said she is no more your sister but till now she is my love don't call her bitch, you bloody fucker and punched him on the mouth.I picked my bag and went away. I am a looser, I lost you my angel, please come back Anadi I can't live without you.

I stopped near a petrol pump and sat at the corner thinking what should I do. A man of age abut 40 years came near me and asked what happen beta; he is wearing a dress of Hindustan Petroleum. I saw towards him and said nothing I just came to give the most important exam of my life and I am failed. He asked from where you had come. I said from Agra, is there any railway station near by from here. He said the nearest railway station is “Hazrat Nizamuddin” in Delhi. How much rent will be there in local till Agra? He said its 70 Rupees. I checked out my wallet it was missing, I checked all my pockets but it is not there. Then I remembered when Akash or Arpit pushed then it would have fell down from my pocket.

The man asked “beta, if don't have any money to go Agra then you had came to right place, I am a tanker driver of petrol and in the morning at 4:00 am I will go to Mathura Refinery, till there I will drop you after that you will manage yourself."

"Thank you uncle from there its 25 km remaining, I will call my friend." The man gets back to his work. I am very hungry as from the early morning I was starving for food and water. I am waiting for the 4:00 am of the morning and slept on the ground itself. The driver woke me up in morning and asked to sit at the parallel to driver seat in the tanker. After 15 minutes again I slept as I am tired so much. When Mathura is about 50 km I called Mukesh to receive me at Mathura refinery. He came on time to receive me; I told him the complete story. He shouted are you mad Arnav, sometimes at the midnight you say I love Ahana and now you are searching Anadi in Noida.

"Mukesh I don't love Ahana, I love only Anadi and really I can't live without her. Mukesh she is my one and only need and wish." He dropped me at my home and I got inside the house.

My mom enquired about my early return."Actually mom the college had first planned to visit two factories. There they changed their programme and visited in only one factory."

"Let's get fresh and come on the dinning table I am making breakfast." My mom said.

While taking the Bath the only thing revolving inside my brain is that, now I have no option to search Anadi.

My days are getting very bad in college, sometimes I think will this last bencher do anything in his life or not, everywhere I miss Anadi too much. When my last semester had started many companies had came for placement, but I am not satisfying there criterion as my overall percentage is 54 %. In few of the companies I am satisfying the criterion and they loved my confidence level but rejected me knowledge wise. The only thing which I have is my communication skill and a high confidence level. After two months my Engineering will be over and I didn't get my love nor do I get a perfect mark sheet in Engineering. I am taking my lecture as usual in the class sitting at the last bench alone. Mukesh and Rahul had improved a lot in studies and got placement in an electronics company of Noida. About 80 % of the students of my class got job before completing the Engineering. The remaining students wants to do further studies and few have them have family business like Astish kaushik, who's father has 3 petrol pump's and 2 gas agencies. Well done Astish god had gifted you not as an Engineer but as a business man. As I am busy in thinking about the placement cell of the college, those found me as a terrorist that's why not selecting me for the job. I am planning to have a dairy farm after completing my Engineering as it's impossible for me to get job. I am planning the name of dairy farm and I said its perfect "Anadi Dairy Farm". And the class gate knocked by a peon of the college, everyone saw towards the gate as we got 2 minutes relaxation in the boring class. The teacher asked what happen "Ramu bhaiya". Some one had came to meet Arnav Sharma and waiting at the main hall. I mumbled, I had not opened the dairy farm and for inauguration party people had started coming. I moved towards the gate of the class. I asked who is there "Ramu Bhaiya". Ramu bhaiya said I don't know go and meet them at the hall. I opened the gate of main hall and saw there is no one in the hall. I closed the door and a voice came from inside of an old man. I suddenly opened the gate and saw at the corner of the hall two people were sitting facing opposite to gate. I came near to them and said "Hello". The old man whose voice I heard had turned towards me, he came near me and while he is coming my eyes are towards the lady sitting quiet till now she had not turned back.

"Hello Arnav, my name is Dr. J. Arun Sharma from Delhi".

"Hello sir, I don't think that we had ever met earlier" and again my eyes moved towards the lady but till now she had not faced back, busy in reading college magazine.

The man replied, "We had met earlier Arnav and I have some thing due on you".

"What due, I had never given you anything," I said.

"You had not given me anything but you had saved my life., how can I forget the one who saved my life?Arnav, about 3.5 years ago at the railway track in Agra my leg was stucked and the train was coming, then you had saved me from that, I think now you remember."

" Yaa, off course, how are you man and after that, I hope you had stop roaming on the track while the gate is closed." I said.

"Yes, Arnav I had stopped, I had came to give you something to complete my due."He said.

"Hey, there is no need of doing any formalities I don't want anything." "Arnav won't you ask how I got your address after a long time.Someone special had told me, he pointed towards that lady, till now she had not faced back." He said.

"let me introduce you to someone special." He said in a loud voice "beti come here".She was hesitating to turn back. She was in saffron color sari. She turned back towards us and my phone start ringing, I had not seen the lady and turned back to receive the phone, it's from Mukesh

"hey who had come and when will you be free?"

I said call you later and disconnected the phone. I turned back towards the lady, I saw that lady and she was my Angel.ANADI. She smiled towards me. I ran towards her and hugged her. We both had tears in our eyes.

"I love you Arnav."

"No you don't Anadi if you had loved me then you would not have left me for so much time."

Arnav I don't had any option, other than that, if I would not have done that then not mine its your life which could have been spoiled and its all because of me. Your parents were not agreeing for marriage and we both are not in condition to have love marriage, you are not stable at that you need your education not me.That's why it's better for me to get bad in front of your eyes than spoiling your life."

"Ohh my baby that's why my heart didn't believe that you had cheated me. Do you know Anadi I had searched you everywhere darling, but I didn't found you, now I will never let you go sweetheart" I kissed on her forehead and said I love you. The man had come near us and said

"hello Mr. Arnav, it's your college not your bed room kindly try to understand and leave Anadi". I left Anadi and gave a tight hug to that man and said thank you so much. The man mumbled towards Anadi "is he gay Anadi". We all trio laughed and moved towards the chairs in the hall.

Anadi told me "on the day of my marriage I had told everything about you in front of all the relatives, Arpit's family rejected me on the spot they took back the barat. My parents told me leave us, as we have no more relation with this girl. I don't have any other option then leaving that place. I had decided to do suicide in front of any vehicle.As the car came near me, I had jumped in front of that.This man was friving the car.I jumped but my luck. Immediately he took me to the hospital and saved my life. I told everything to him, he told me to live with him as a daughter. I told him that I don't want to be burden on you. Then he had given me a job in his hospital and yesterday in evening I told him about you and your entire incident, everything about you, that once you had saved someone's life. After hearing this he had taken me to meet you. Arnav if I am standing in front of you then it's because of this man, he is much more than god for me. Arnav I had not came here to disturb your life. Till evening we will get back to Delhi. This man wanted to meet you once and he had not seen your college. He had come to say thank you."

The man said, "if you love each other then why don't you marry."

"my parents didn't agree for other caste girl and moreover I am not stable, I don't have any job till now. And the simple thing I don't want to insult my parents because of me. My parent's wants arrange marriage."

The man said "I have a solution of all your problems, if you both cooperate with me. Arnav your college will be over with in 15 minutes, lets move to a restaurant there we will decide for the next step." I called Mukesh and said that I am leaving college with my relative's for home. I was wondering how was he going to help me with such low academic record and my strict parents.

He had a car. He called his driver to come with the car. With in a minute a white color Mercedes Benz had come and it stopped near us. The driver has a better uniform then my college uniform. First time I sat in mercedez,I am busy in seeing the interior.

I asked "so you are a doctor." Anadi interrupted in between and said he has his own three personal hospitals.

"Wow, how you manage this sir, how many son or daughter do you have?" Anadi again interrupted and said "Sir do not have any child, he lives with his wife alone".

"Ohh I am sorry sir."

"Now I have 2 childrens. You both" We both smiled and agreed.

The driver had parked car in front of 5-star hotel. We came out of the car, I picked Anadi's hand. The man saw towards me and said don't worry she will not leave you alone. Anadi smiled and said he is correct Arnav, I am always yours. We moved to the restaurant section. We had chosen the center table of the restaurant. It was a set of three chairs. We sat on the chair and the man said that my life will change soon.I didn't understand anything.He picked his mobile from the pocket and called a number. He starts talking in complete English language. He is talking about a job of some one and he suddenly disconnects the phone.

"Arnav do you want to job in India or out side India." I was shocked.

"I want to see outside India." I somehow replied. He called his driver and asked him to bring his laptop. The driver brings the laptop and the man had sent a mail. Then he asked me do you have resume.

I said yes on my email id, I had saved. He said, I just want to send your resume at this id. I opened my email id and sent my resume to that id. After I send a resume, with in 30 seconds the man's phone rang. He received the call and after some conversation he said thank you to the opposite person on phone. The man disconnect the phone and said after 4 months you have a joining in a multinational company in U.S.A as a production engineer, all your document will be received by you with in 5 days. I am shocked, what the fuck is going all this?

I stood up and said "sorry sir but I don't want your help regarding my job. Thank you for saving my Anadi and helping her till now. But know leave me and Anadi."

Anadi shouted "what are you saying Arnav, this man is helping us and you are shouting on him."

"Anadi you are with me or with that man, I had not taken any help of anyone and will not take any help." The man stood up and said "hey Arnav I know that your self respect is lot important, but who said I am doing charity on you I am just giving you a reward for saving my life, it's a gift to you from destiny for your goodwill work towards me". Anadi kept her hand on my cheeks and said "Arnav there is nothing we are doing, everything is happening what the destiny is written".

I said "ok, what you will do next." He took my mobile and took my dad's number. He called my dad and said, "You are Mr. Arnav's father speaking". The man had switched on the speaker of his mobile. My father replied "yes, I am."

"Sir my name is Dr. J. Arun Sharma, just now I got news that your son is going to complete his engineering with in 2 months and got a job in U.S.A. as a production engineer in a multinational company, I want to marry your son with my daughter Anadi Sharma. My father said from where you are calling sir. He said I am calling from Delhi and I am a doctor from profession, Anadi is my single daughter. I saw your son's photograph and complete bios ketch on matrimonials.com. My complete family had liked Arnav and we are ready to marry, we want you to see our daughter if you are interested in continuing relation with us. My father said, first I will ask from my family and Arnav after that I will say anything. The man said ok, sir take your time I will wait for your call and he disconnect the phone.

I said "if my family get ready to see Anadi then they will catch her that she is Anadi Gupta not Anadi Sharma."

" Don't worry for that I had planned to do plastic surgery on Anadi's cheeks, it's mostly a 1 hour work and no one will understand with different cheeks.

The man and Anadi left for Delhi.I reached home and saw my father had came back from his job and sitting on the dining table with mom. I smiled and said "what a surprise dad; you are here without any call or message." "This surprise doesn't matter Arnav but the surprise you had given of your job in U.S.A. is much bigger." He hugged me and congratulated me. I asked from where you know that I got a job."I was very happy.

"What do you think; we don't have any link for our son. He said son tomorrow we had planned to see a girl for your marriage in Delhi. If you don't mind will you go?" I mumbled planned had work, I said "dad my marriage decision will be yours, I know that you will not do take wrong step for me". My father said thanks beta for believing us.

Next morning my mom and dad had move for Delhi, it will take 4 hours to reach, till then everything will be arranged there in Delhi by Anadi. I am waiting for dad and mom in the evening, Anadi is not receiving my call, I am scared that it might some tragedy had taken place. And the gate knocks, I seen from the window it was dad and mom. I opened the gate and asked to my mom, what happen how's the family and how's the girl? Arnav do you know the girls father is a doctor and have three hospitals, they are really very rich. I don't know how they had found the address of our middle class people. My mom said "anyways, they are very good and the girl is very beautiful and kindhearted, I liked her lot. I had saved one photo in my mobile."

I opened the photo from my mom's mobile and saw Anadi's face is changed after plastic surgery, she is looking more beautiful then earlier. My dad said "we had fixed the marriage after 2.5 months on 20th June. Till then you will complete all your exams of your last semester."

I called Anadi and said "hey congratulations your marriage is been fixed." She replied "you too my sweetheart."

"Anadi had you ever thought of this day ever, for me its all miracle."

"Arnav I don't know about it but every day after I had come from Agra I had missed u a lot darling. My day starts with you that how's Arnav this time. My every breath is connected to the name Arnav, I love you Arnav."

"I love you too Anadi. In college not even a single day or single second had passed without you."

Now my complete routine is changed of day and night. Most of the time I am online with Anadi as know she was going to be my legal wife.

After 2.5 months, 20th June

Every one is ready at my house for the barat. My father had booked two air condition buses for the relatives. We reached Delhi at the hotel in the evening about 4 o'clock. Everyone is mad after getting down from the bus to the hotel in dancing style; my dad had arranged the band. The hotel which is booked by my genuine father in law is a 5star hotel. After seeing the hotel and the arrangement all my relatives had start talking with their jealousy feelings. Sometimes these jealousy feelings give relax to the heart as everything is going good. My father in law had played all the roles in a very good manner with her wife means my mother in law is too with him while the rules and regulation. My law had invited mostly unknown persons as his relatives in the marriage so that no one gives hindrance in between the marriage that who is that girl? My relatives are busy in knowing more and more about my in laws with their relatives who is been invited by in laws but they are not satisfy with anyone as the one whom they met is his friend. At last every thing get success my in laws had made their dreams true of children and I had made my dream true as Anadi's husband. We came back from Delhi to our home in the next morning. Everyone is happy with the marriage but every relative is confused that Arnav's in laws has mostly invited his friend not his relatives. But the one in between all the relative the super senior might be anyone says big people do not have so many contacts. They use feel and live free that's why they didn't get in contact more with them. After 10 days I received two tickets to U.S.A. and a joining letter of the company. At the airport my parents and my in laws had came to c-off us. Anadi had made them too much close with her as its impossible to say that they are not her parents. We had settled in U.S.A. in a very short period of time. In a year one time we use to go India and two times my in laws use to come U.S.A. For the whole world it had shown that Sharma boy had marriage a Sharma girl. But in real, two true lovers had made their destiny by their own. Most of the love story end at the caste problem some of them found out their solution but some of them didn't made their dreams true with their partners everyone has different conditions some of them are favorable and some are unfavorable. But everything depends on destiny. The thing which is written in destiny will happen if it is not, no one can make it happen. As in today's era mostly the people has started thinking about love of college life is that it is fuck and forget, but it seems to be wrong many times.

Back to the bus

"Hey, wake up Shiel boring story is finish and Roorkee is going to come with in 10 minutes."

"Don't say this how can I sleep while listening so much interesting story, so the first question is how is Anadi?" I said.

"She is fine and lives in U.S.A. and now she is a teacher in a school there." Arnav said.

"Wow, she is good. Arnav after listening to your story I believe in love and destiny too much."

Conductor signaled the passengers for Roorkee leave their place and arrange their luggage, we will wait only 2 minutes,I and Arnav stood up to arrange the luggage, got down to the bus on Roorkee bus stand.

"So where will you stay shiel do you have some residence or will stay in a hotel." Arnav asked.

"I had planned to live in a hotel," I said.

"Let's go I will show you the perfect hotel, I am also going to stay in that," Arnav said.

"Hey are you going to stay in the hotel, whose money you had stolen? You can be caught by the owner," I warned.

"Don't worry its long time ago he is not going to remember me and I have to stay here only for two days."

We both are standing in front of hotel "Man Singh Hotel", I was afraid and was trying to convince arnav to move to some other place. But he forced me to stay there itself. We knocked on the counter,

"yes, what do you want?"

Arnav said we want one single room for two people. Arnav mumbled he is the owner of the hotel; I am in his touch mostly.

"I don't know but I am feeling that I had seen you earlier," the man said.

I interrupted and said, we had came here just for the first time can you please show us the room fast.

"definitely Sir".

He showed us the room and we got settled in that.

"sorry Shiel without asking to you I had chosen that we would live together, if you have some problem then I will leave this room now."

"Hey Arnav what are you saying? You had shared me your life and now I am your part of life." I said.

Whole day and night had passed over. I did not leave Arnav for a single moment, every time I used to ask different questions about his life.

Next day morning he woke me up at 8:00 am and said "let's go to the coaching from tomorrow you have the classes and today have to do registration process."

We reached coaching classes.the first man we met is the same teacher with whom Arnav has to meet.

"Hello, sir good morning!"

The teacher said "hey you Arnav how you had come here? Want to do again Embedded system as you had not completed the last time."

"No, sir I had completed everything in the course but do you remember the challenge you had given to me?"

"YesI do"

"So sir I want to show your resume". Arnav had shown his resume to the teacher. After seeing the resume his company name which is in U.S.A. he is shocked and unable to answer anything.

"Sir I had came here to insult you I had came here to tell that there is nothing written in your hand for having bright future of any child. The student itself is the owner of himself, if you will try to force him or judge him then it is useless until the student itself doesn't want to do anything, no one can do anything."

"So Arnav you had win the challenge, what do you want?" The teacher said.

"Sir I don't want anything I just want to feel you that there is nothing going to happen if you will admit your mistake in front of student."

After saying this Arnav and I moved to the administration room for my registration. After registration Arnav had planned to get back to Agra.

I took all his contact number, email address and his house address. I had tried to stop Arnav for few days but he said I have some work in Agra.

He took the bus for Agra and I had gone back to my room. I asked to the counter of my hotel about the total amount of money. He said, the bill is already paid last night by your big brother.

After hearing about the bill paid I suddenly called Arnav, but the number is not available. I had tried many times to contact Arnav through the information given by him but all the information were faulty.